For Tom Hay, friend
and fellow-laborer
from

Joe Hopkins

8/31/60

RETREAT AND RECALL

Books by Joseph G. E. Hopkins

RETREAT AND RECALL

PATRIOT'S PROGRESS

RETREAT
AND
RECALL

By JOSEPH G. E. HOPKINS

CHARLES SCRIBNER'S SONS, New York

PRINTED IN THE UNITED STATES OF AMERICA

Library of Congress Catalog Card Number 66-16690

CONTENTS

I wish to be useful, and every kind of service, necessary to the public good, becomes honorable by being necessary.

Nathan Hale

I

NEW YORK:
THE FORT AND
THE PRISON

November and December, 1776

CHAPTER ONE

FROM THE rampart where he stood near the north-west angle of the fort, a wall of hard-packed earth fell sheer for some twenty feet. Close by the base of the wall, the ground began a steep descent to the shore of the Hudson and a narrow path twisted down through rocks and trees and brushwood to the cove where the transport boats came in from Jersey. Beyond the broad river and the westward cliffs, the sky was streaked and pied with sunset light. Fingers of shadow lengthened out over the water downstream until they touched the enemy ships at anchor under furled canvas. The assault would begin at a little after dawn, he thought. For wars were fought by changeless rule, as the games of children are played.

The watcher on the wall was only of middling height but he was young and strongly made. The sun and wind had browned his skin to a look of health and vigor yet his blue eyes stared out from dark pools of weariness in his thin, plain face. His name was John Frayne; he was a native of Wendham in Massachusetts and a surgeon in the army of America. Until lately, he had been serving in the hospital at Hackensack in Jersey. A week since, on the eighth day of November, 1776, he had been ordered here to Fort Washington on the island of Manhattan.

When the minuteman company of Wendham had marched off to Concord in a bright April morning, their captain, the town blacksmith Abijah Flagg, had begged him to go with them. Neither conviction nor ardor had persuaded him. The loud, pot-valiant brag of the common sort of people, whenever they met to protest against Parliament or to scribble out lengthy memorials to the Congress, had amused him for a time and at last wearied him. He had never supposed that their play at politics would pit them against the King's soldiers. His first thought when Abijah summoned him was wonder; the next was an overwhelming pity for poor, foolish men who marched to their certain destruction. He owed them nothing. Their leveling principles were alien to all that he believed in and cherished; they had called him a Tory and briefly imprisoned him; they had driven his brother Richard into exile—yet they were men and he was a physician.

The events of that day twenty months before remained fixed in his memory as a sequence of pictures, stark as the copperplate cuts in a child's primer. The headlong march in the dust and heat; the redcoats in flight down the Concord road; the running and shooting and dropping into cover on the hot pursuit to Lexington; the writhing wounded and the quiet dead! That woeful day had lessoned him in life and duty, had rid his mind of cant as the burning brand had cleansed the prophet's mouth. What he had thought to be his habit of reason and conscience and proper pride had been revealed to him in its true light as a coward's fear of failure and loss. No man, he had learned, may stand aside from life or refuse commitment to just and weighty causes. The British had forced a fight upon America and they must be made to rue it. In such a mood of anger and protest, he had joined the army before Boston.

Since that time, he had discovered subtler and deeper motives for his rebellion. He had served with all manner of men at Boston siege, and later at New York—gentle and common, rich and poor, learned and unlettered. "We are Americans," they had told him, "—a new people. We shall govern ourselves under God in all our native concerns, just as our fathers did. We wish only what is due us under the natural law and the laws of the God of nature. We fight to defend our rights and to secure ourselves in future. All mankind will be our debtors for what we do." Stated with more art in the July declaration by the Congress, this creed had been accepted by the greater part of the army. Although it was but ill-sensed by many, it had steeled the wills of Yorkers and Virginians to the work in hand, just as it had persuaded John's own New England people and himself. His older prejudices had slowly withered away and he had taken up his new faith with a zeal which Parson Ithiel Havens had never been able to quicken in Wendham meetinghouse. He had only one regret in all this—a broken promise—but he had schooled himself not to think of it.

A scuff of feet from behind him broke in upon his thoughts and he turned quickly about. A meager, hook-nosed man was clambering up from the firestep. It was Alexander Hearn, the surgeon to Cadwalader's Pennsylvania regiment.

"The drugs are packed and ready," announced the

newcomer. "I'm thankful for them, sir, and for the lint."

"We're scant of supplies ourselves, or I'd have given you more."

"Nay, you've been bounty itself," replied Hearn. "Since we lost our own medicine chest on Long Island, I've had nothing—not so much as a dose of jalap." He stopped to cough, a deep, racking paroxysm. "You never went needy in Jersey, I'll wager," he went on with a sour look. "Trust John Morgan to favor the hospitals. 'Tis shameful! Now that you're on field duty yourself, you'll see how he grinds us regimental surgeons. I hear that Congress means to replace him with a new medical director. *Adsit omen,* by the Eternal! Stringer or Shippen would be my choice, and the sooner the better." Turning away as John offered to speak, he looked down into the body of the fort where a thousand men and more were sprawled beside their evening fires. "How quiet they keep," he said.

"They have the morrow to think of."

"So they have." Hearn shivered and pulled the collar of his coat up about his neck. "I'm no warrior, Frayne. I despise all this."

"And so do I. Yet we've our duty to do."

"We'd a lesson in duty this morning at roll-call." Hearn's voice was somber. "They read us the Colonel's reply to the British summons. 'Colonel Robert Magaw assures General Howe that he will defend Fort Washington to the last extremity.' So it ended, very noble and elegant, like a speech out of Plutarch."

"Do you doubt what he said?"

"I doubt he can do it." Hearn laughed without mirth.

Taking John by the arm, he led him along the rampart to where a view opened southward over the trees.

"Judge our case for yourself," said Hearn, pointing out to the left. "See those fires on the bluff! That's our line of defense on the south. That's where we Pennsylvanians lie—eight hundred of us—with one six-pounder mounted on trucks and a few old iron pieces ready to burst. Lord Percy fronts us with four British regiments and three of Germans. Over there on the east, where the enemy's massing to cross the Harlem, we've a single earthwork on Laurel Hill and a rabble of militia to man it. Rawlings's regiment and one poor battery stand between us and five thousand Hessians at the north by Kingsbridge. And that's the round of the compass, sir, for their warships ply in the Hudson. Defend this miserable den? Impossible. Caesar couldn't defend it, nor Marlborough. It was lost a week ago. We're in a trap, and tomorrow will see it sprung."

"The generals cannot think so. They sent us militia from Jersey only this morning."

"Bad coin after good." Hearn coughed again and spat. "Don't you know the game? The Congress calls the tune here. Our rulers require a Thermopylae—a stand of heroes against odds. They've had naught to brag of but trouble since they voted independence last July—a shambles on Long Island, sad tidings from the lakes and Canada, a bare escape at the White Plains! So we must set the country an example. What matter if the fort must fall and we be killed or captivated? The most of the army lies safe in Westchester and Jersey—and we shall have ballads made of us."

"A betrayal? You're daft."

"As you please." Hearn shrugged his thin shoulders. "We'll talk of it later—in a British prison, if we're lucky. Generals, say you? Who are they? Save for George Washington, not a single first man of Virginia or New England stands at the head of troops. Schoolmasters lead us—farmers, debtors, horse-breakers, fortune-seekers. I saw your famous Israel Putnam today. He came over from Fort Lee in Jersey to study our lines. And a rare sight he was, in an old ragged coat with an old rusty hanger belted on him and a swagger in his walk like the chief of a band of harvest-hands. No wonder that our rank-and-file are the worst of the common sort."

"I marvel that you stay with us then," said John, at once angry and concerned. Hearn made him no answer for a time but stood staring out over the darkening woods.

"I stay because I must," he replied at last. "'Tis a fool's reason, after all I've seen since I left Philadelphia, but there's no help for it. Our cause is good, no matter how base its champions may be. And now I'll be off to my post," he ended, more briskly. "God speed you, Frayne. And my thanks for the medicines once again."

A fool's reason, to be sure, thought John as he watched Hearn go. The fellow was confident indeed if he believed that any cause could be abstracted wholly from those who led and fostered it. Its glory was theirs and they could lend it infamy as well. If he were ever to think as Hearn did, the army would soon be scant a surgeon.

The camp fires had dwindled to glowing heaps of coals by the time John descended from the rampart to the open parade. Except for the men on guard duty, the troops lay wakeful by their arms or tossed in restless sleep as he picked his way among them to the open-fronted wooden hut that served the fort for a hospital. It was all his own now. Late the last evening, James Mc-Henry, the surgeon to Magaw's regiment with whom he had shared it, had gone to the eastern outpost on Laurel Hill. His two mates—Gillespie, a sharp lad from the North End of Boston, and Mason, a broad-faced, ambling put from Connecticut—lay snoring on the straw-strewn floor of the hut but no sick were within. Along with the soldiers' wives and the camp-followers, they had all been sent to refuge in Newark and Hackensack and other of the Jersey towns.

John tried to sleep but he could not. His visitor's dismal talk still rang in his ears and awakened doubts more troubling than the noise of the guard on rounds or the distant rumble of enemy wheels.

Fort Washington was a shell of mud, three hundred feet on a side; it lacked bomb-proofs, ditches and screening out-works. It had no well; the men must fetch water in from the Hudson, or from a spring that lay at a perilous distance beyond the north gate. Its site, high up on beetling rocks, was a point of strength, yet the guns looked out through shallow ports at stands of trees that would make a perfect cover for the besiegers. A row of horse-sheds along the inside of the western wall and the squat powder-magazine, half-buried in earth, were its principal structures. Here and there along the parade, and in no apparent order, a quantity of military stores lay heaped under canvas coverings. The more fortunate of the garrison sheltered in tents made of sailcloth (the Colonel himself making shift for quarters in a tent near the hospital hut), but the greater number slept in their blankets on the cold ground and exposed to the four winds of heaven.

A scarecrow fort it was indeed, and worth not a rush so long as the British remained masters of the rest of Manhattan. Yet men would die in its defense. For some strategic purpose? Or to salve the hurt pride of Congress?

Rising from the straw, John went out of the hut and began to pace swiftly before it. If Hearn spoke truth, this war might settle a worse tyranny than Parliament's on America—a native junto of crafty cowards who ventured brave men's lives like pennies in play. But why was Hearn's charge against Congress any worthier of belief than his slurs on the medical director? These were mere railing and slander, as John well knew. The regimental surgeons had been damning John Morgan for months, out of malice chiefly and self-conceit because he had dealt sternly with them. No man of sense could propose to replace him with Samuel Stringer or William Shippen. The army in Canada had rotted of small-pox under Stringer's care, and Shippen was a brilliant marplot still bitter with a grudge he bore Morgan over credit for founding the medical college in Philadelphia. He would stop at nothing to even the score. The tale that the director hoarded medicines in the general hospital was a lie of Shippen's minting.

The wind stirred cold. John clutched his cloak tightly about him. At home in Massachusetts, the farmers would have looked long since to their barns and folds and the goodwives have taken their potted slips and simples to a place in the warmest kitchen window. Soon the great gusts would beat against farmhouse and town house, roaring bleak over the frozen ponds and marshes; soon the deep snows would fall. Far over the sheeted fields, the crows would sweep in harsh-voiced flight. Out beyond in the woods the preying kind would be lurking, the owls and the hawks.

The small world of his youth was suddenly quick in his mind's eye, as on the day he had left it; he saw the High Street between the leafing elms, Jos Cushing's store and the drowsing teams outside it, the meeting-house brooding over the green, the clapboarded tavern where his mother kept. His surgery too—the low, long room in the tavern ell with the tall press against the wall and the rows of drawers and vials and China jars; the well-conned volumes of Boerhaave and Cullen; the lamplight on the green cloth of the table as he sat to his studies after a hard day's practice. He heard the dogs bark in the evening quiet and the voices of townsmen going home from the taproom, the daytime hum of trade in the south-end lanes, the fall of the sledge at Flagg's forge, the lowing of cattle on a market day.

And faces arose in his fancy as well, some from his boyhood yet the most from the near past. Abijah Flagg's, as coarse and honest as oak, Ben Ripley's, and many another of those good comrades in arms who had taught him his duty that day of Concord fight by word and deed—or by their death, like the Stoddards, Hugh and Seth, and Increase Hammond. And Alison Cunningham's face.

But it was his father's image that persisted as he strode back and forth before the hospital hut—his father's care-worn, innocent face, now bending over a sickbed, now smiling with proud pleasure as his son grew skillful in

their art. He heard his father's voice again, discoursing
on their work as they rode abroad in all weathers, speaking of politics too at times, urging his skeptic philosophy
most of all. "Take no side, boy, in any cause. Submit all
things to reason. Be too proud ever to be hustled into an
opinion. You'll never be disappointed then."

Good counsel for a tranquil time, thought John, but
not for all of life. Pride and reason did not always avail.
They failed a man in love and death, the two things
paramount in his earthly passage. He had put love aside,
to be sure, but death had still to be reckoned with. If he
should fall on the morrow, what would remain of him?
Only the memory of his father's son, a recollection of
one who had practiced the art of medicine indifferent
well and had come to know himself too late—one who
had served no great purpose or achieved any single
thing of the least importance.

He stood stock-still in the cold, considering the likeli-
hood of his own death as he had considered it many
times before, not fearful in the vulgar way but troubled
and heavy of heart.

From the shadow of the hut, a deeper shadow moved
toward him.

" 'Tis I, Gillespie," whispered the mate's voice. "Cannot you sleep, sir? Neither can I."

"You'd best attempt it," John answered sharply.
"Tomorrow will be no May game."

"Aye, I know it. I was thinking how many poor lads
won't see the sun go down."

John was no longer surprised at sensibility in the
common sort of men, as he had been once.

" 'Tis a pity, truly," he answered in a kindlier tone, "yet there's no help for it."

"Are ye no afeared?" Gillespie's voice was wondering and respectful. "I am. I'm like to wilt right down."

"We're all afraid unless we're fools. The British too."

"It's only of late that I've been fearful. When I jined up at Boston, I was spilin' to fight the lobsters and the Tories. Besides that, the shipyards was idle and there wan't any work. Now that we've been sojerin' all this time with naught to show but knocks, I hear tell from home that the yards is busy again. Every caulker and wright has a handsome wage, so they say—and I'm damned if I wants to die so's they can get rich."

It was a fair hit, thought John, remembering his last visit to Wendham on leave from Boston siege. The town Committeemen had not waited for opportunity; they had forced it. Others might do the work and fight the battles, but the profits of army contracts and sequestered Tory estates were already chinking in the pockets of Chairman Joel Gay and his fellow politicians.

"We've the rights of America in our keeping," he said, however. "We've our duty to do. If others skulk and hide at home, we're not excused because they're conscienceless."

"Maybe, maybe." Gillespie pondered the matter a little. "Yet it's cruel hard that they should frolic whilst we must fight."

John had no answer to that. Even as he had been speaking, he had recognized how trite and pompous his words were, how inadequate to express what he truly felt. With sudden compunction, he recalled Hearn's final speech to him on the rampart. He had thought it a foolish speech, yet his own must ring as false to Gillespie now.

"Good night to ye, sir," said the mate, turning away towards the hut. "I'll try again to sleep."

"Good night."

How could any man acquaint another with his convictions, derived as they were through tortuous processes of thought and experience and given life by a myriad considerations which the other could not know or guess at? Why was he, John Frayne, striding about here in the dark and cold and awaiting a day whose issue might well be fatal? There were reasons for it beyond reason, motives of which he was himself only intuitively aware, an ancestral dictation which could not be brooked or denied. Duty was all; once seen and known, there was no escaping it for his father's son.

CHAPTER TWO

EARLY IN the spring of 1774, John's father, Peter
Frayne, had died possessed of the love and respect
of every poor creature in the county of Suffolk, and of
an estate not worth the costs of probate. Few physicians
in his time had been more skillful than Peter Frayne,
but he was happier in serving men than in taking their
money, and happiest when he could find an audience
for his speculations on the great ends of life and the
promises of science. In all of this he was a true type of
his race, for he was descended of a line of clergymen and
physicians long established in the Province of Massachusetts, learned men and kindly, liberal of mind and
purse, and knowing no let to their thought and actions
save reason and conscience.

John's mother was sprung of a very different strain,
the Allens of Ipswich—a notable clergy family also, but
as apt in all practical concerns as the Fraynes were heedless. Soon after her marriage, when it became plain to
her that her husband was wedded first to philosophy,
Elizabeth Frayne laid out her family portion in the purchase of the Vernon Arms at Wendham and stayed her

declining fortunes by her prosperous conduct of that inn. As year succeeded year, her husband's unthrifty ways aggravated her already severe nature into harshness of spirit, miserliness, and envy of the more fortunate. The lowered respect which was paid her because of her tavern-keeping fretted her pride, and she looked to her sons for revival of the family credit in a world increasingly managed by merchants, lawyers, and the like inferior people.

John Frayne had grown to manhood, therefore, in a divided and uneasy household. His mother's constant effort to school him in the world's ways as a counter to his father's weakness (for so she styled his charity and devotion to knowledge), so vexed and disgusted John that he mistook her for a cold, unfeeling woman. He remained unaware of the true cast of her mind until the day he went off to the army, when her revelation of tender concern surprised him more than it gratified him. For the time had gone by for tenderness between them. She had made his life a course of denials and disappointments and him a stoic, proud, withdrawn into himself, and scornful of all enthusiasms.

His brother had always appeared their mother's favorite. Richard was a wit, well-favored, quick at his studies, and gifted with a talent for screening his thoughts behind smiling grey eyes and under light and artful speech. In the storms that swept the family, he could bend whilst John stood stubborn. Following John to Harvard College, he had graduated with honor a short time after their father's death. He had then become master of the Wendham school. John, meanwhile, had spent three years in the study of medicine with his father after his own graduation from Harvard in 1771, and had succeeded to the practice in Wendham.

His life, beyond his professional duties, had been uneventful. Denied the opportunity to study over sea at Edinburgh or Leyden, he had resigned himself to his country practice, recovering his ambitions over his books on those rare evenings when a day's rounds had not spent him. Although he was convinced that both sides were at fault in the great contest over taxes, he preferred the errors of a tried if imperfect government of gentlemen in London to the promises of a set of Boston spouters and demagogues. The outcry of the popular Committees at what they called the tyranny of King George and his ministers of state aroused in him only contempt. As much of pride and old gentility supported this opinion as of loyalty to the Crown, for the patriot Committeemen of Wendham and its neighborhood were mere farmers and mechanics, men of no worth, and led by the blackleg horse-trader Joel Gay.

There was little to choose, in all truth, between the contending factions. The King's chief friend in Wendham was Thomas Cunningham, called Squire Cunningham by his debtors and by the common sort of people. An attorney once, he had become a successful trader in rum, iron and black men out of Newport in Rhode Island, and was latterly a landowner, usurer, and justice of the peace. In all his undertakings he had shown himself a selfish, cold-blooded projector, purse-proud, arrogant when he dared, and a type of the newly rich. On his settling at Wendham in 1770, he had built himself a splendid house to the westward of the town green. His only daughter, Alison, had come there to live with him in 1772. Her mother had died when she was but a small girl and she had been reared by her aunts in Boston until her sixteenth year.

Her coming marked a climacteric for John; he had loved her from his first sight of her. He had peopled his loneliness with her image, delighting in her delicacy of figure and grace of motion, in the quick come-and-go of color beneath her pale skin, in the play of expression across her springtime face. She was a dark beauty, her features as fine and chastely modeled as those of some nymph or dryad on an antique gem but lively and prideful too, and with a curious, wistful look sometimes as of one waiting for she knew not what. Try as he would to account for it, the secret of her attraction eluded him. It was a general harmony of being, more than any specific perfections—an air which she diffused about her like a perfume which was she and no other. For whatever reason, he was her slave and happy to be so. Despite her father's ambitions for a wealthy son-in-law with a title perchance in prospect, despite his own stiff self-esteem which kept him for a long time silent in fear of a rebuff, she had loved him for a little. She had promised herself to him and they were to have been wed. But it had all come to nothing.

The fault had been his as much as hers.

On the 16th of April, 1775, a Sabbath day, the patriot Committee of Wendham had roused up the common folk against Thomas Cunningham and had confined him and his daughter to their house under guard as malignant Tories. The Committee had also denounced Richard Frayne and others in the town, but Richard, who had been deep engaged in a belated opposition of loyal men to the popular movement, had managed to escape arrest. He had fled first to Boston and thence to London, where he was now (or so John had heard) a poor, scribbling drudge for one of the ministerial journals.

By the favor of some of her captors and by bribery of others, Alison Cunningham had contrived a flight to Boston and the protection of the British arms. She had settled on Wednesday, the 19th of April, for the escape and John had promised to go with her and her father.

That Wednesday morning seemed as remote as childhood now. The air, crystalline after a night of rain, had turned soft and warm by nine o'clock; it had been a day fitter for musing and repose than for action or for the heavy thoughts that oppressed John while he waited outside his surgery door. The intended flight must surely appear a desertion of his mother in a dangerous time, yet he had given his word to go. Moreover, his best hopes were bound up in the adventure. He and Alison would wed as soon as they arrived safe in Boston and his career would be furthered through the Squire's interest with the royal officials. No harm would come to his mother, he told himself; she had wit and will enough to carry her securely even through war and revolution. But his hopes and his scruples were alike forgot when a horseman rode at a gallop down High Street, crying the news of Lexington.

The Wendham minutemen and the reserve company had formed ranks before the tavern—a sad, unhandy crew in all truth, hectored into a show of discipline by Abijah Flagg and by their lieutenant Cullen, John's mother's Irish groom and a deserter from the Boston garrison. Carried away by his own sensibility, John had marched with them.

He had served before Boston until the fall of that city in March, 1776. The Wendham company was soon assigned to a regiment already provided with surgeons, so he had enrolled as a volunteer with Gridley's artillery. After his commissioning on the army establishment, he had been ordered to the general hospital at Cambridge.

Each time a post-bag passed the siege lines at Roxbury, he had addressed a letter to Alison within the city. They had been humble, remorseful letters, begging her forgiveness for his broken word to her, and urging on her how conscience and professional honor had compelled his action. No answer had ever come. Desperate at last, he had entered Boston in disguise at the risk of his neck. She had received him with scorn for his desertion of her and for his treason to the King. In the end, however, she had confessed to another reason for her rejection of his pleas. Her father's narrowed circumstances and her own ambition had brought her to accept the protection of one Stanhope Damer, a dragoon officer of the British garrison and a peer's son. He had promised her marriage. John had begged her to reconsider, to forgive him and to wait for him. The city would soon be taken, he had told her. He would make all right. But she had promised nothing.

A month later, entering Boston with the first of the American troops, he had sought her out only to find that she had sailed to Halifax with Damer and her father.

Early in April he had marched with the army to New London in Connecticut, whence they had completed the journey to New York by ship. He had been witness to all the woes of the army since; he had watched it ravaged by disease, routed by the British on Long Island, driven from Kip's Bay. And now he awaited the dawn of a Thermopylae, as Hearn had described it—a stand against hopeless odds. Please God, it would serve some purpose.

His thoughts turned to Alison again. Her image was never far from his recollection and was ever the same, just as he had seen her last in Boston, looking down over the stair-rail in Stanhope Damer's house. The lamp she held had glimmered on her damask gown and on her dark, curling hair; the gown had been blue like her eyes, a deep blue like hyacinths. Was she in Halifax now? Damer had taken her there on one of the refugee ships but they would not have tarried long in that dismal place. No, she was in London more likely, a great lady as her ambition had pictured her to herself, and Damer's wife.

There was anger in his thought of her now, as well as pity and hurt. "Remember me as I seemed to you," she had told him that night in Boston. "I was never what you thought me." She was right. Better to cherish an illusion of lost, innocent times than to torture himself as he had been doing since the day of the city's fall. She had made her choice, as he had. Whatever her fate might be, it no longer concerned him. Fort Washington must stand an assault in a few hours. That was fact. All else was dream.

He went back into the hut and stretched himself out

again on the bed of straw. The mates were learning fast, he thought; Gillespie was a deft hand at bandaging and might do more in time. From a long way off, as it seemed, he heard the challenges of the guard along the walls, post after post replying. And then he slept.

CHAPTER THREE

H E WOKE before dawn; his bones were aching with cold. Rising, he swung his arms to set the blood in motion and he stamped his tingling feet. The air smelled of mould and damp.

He roused up his mates and put them to work. Soon, a fire was blazing under the great water caldron within the hut, the table for amputations was fixed firm on its trestles, and fresh straw had been shaken out where the wounded would lie. By the time the drum beat reveille, all was in readiness but it was pitifully little—barely enough for the accidents of a muster-day, let alone a battle and a siege. Moreover, the men were too close confined in this place and the fogs from the river were pernicious. He would have fever to deal with if the siege were long drawn-out.

"You, Gillespie—and you too, Mason," he called to the mates, "stand by me here for practice. Let's say I must take off a leg below the knee. How will you staunch the bleeding?"

The garrison was forming on the parade; the lines faced inward around three sides of a square. After roll-call, the captains began inspection of the companies, looking in particular to the set of flints and the contents of cartridge boxes. Then they dressed ranks again and an officer read out the orders of the day in a high, nasal voice.

"Load with one ball for the first fire. Add a mite of buckshot too—four to eight of 'em, so many as yer piece'll take. If the enemy tries a storm, hold fire 'til he's at the mark—that's the line we've drawn outside on the cleared ground—"

The cannoneers were sighting along the barrels of their guns—12- and 32-pounders mainly—raising or depressing the muzzles a fraction of an inch. A file of matrosses passed powder buckets hand-to-hand from the magazine to the firesteps.

"Every third man'll be served out a pike," the nasal voice continued. "They do fine agin bayonets. Fatigue companies, fall out now and fill up the water kegs!"

The relieving guard companies moved forward to their posts; the off-duty men were dismissed. A vast hum arose, and a noise of axe blows, as the soldiers built up the fires and set about making their breakfasts.

"This here sea-bread—" complained a man near by John. "You call this fitten food? 'Twould bust the teeth of a rat."

Nothing could make the ration palatable, not even the issue of rum, thought John in sympathy. He had no desire for such food now, nor the time to forage for better. Salt meat and sea-bread! And the rich farms of Jersey and Westchester almost in sight from the ramparts! Here was slackness again, and something worse—indifference. That self-same want of forethought which had left him without blankets for the wounded, which forced him to improvise splints out of bits of twig. He cursed aloud.

The mates, attentive to his lesson in bandaging a shoulder, looked up in surprise for he was not given to swearing. He made them no explanation and went on with his work, but he was conscious of their stares.

The British were tardy. It was past dawn now; it was coming light.

"Here's someone to speak you, cap'n," Gillespie said.

John faced angrily about. The fire under the boiling caldron glinted on a scarlet uniform coat; its wearer stepped forward into the hut, bowing as he came and taking off his hat. He murmured something, but in a voice too low to be understood.

"Speak up, man! We have business here."

The stranger's tall figure stiffened but he showed no other resentment.

"Do I address the surgeon of the post?" he asked, still softly, and hesitantly as if his words required careful choosing. "I am James Shawcross, sir—lieutenant in the Maryland battalion. We lie at the small redoubt on the height over Kingsbridge." He fell silent then, his shoulders stooping like one who expects a blow. At closer view, he was unshaven and pale; his coat was weather-stained and torn in several places.

"I beg your indulgence for coming at such a time," he began again, "but I must have your help. I—I—" His voice trailed off. His eyes did not meet John's but were fixed straight ahead and staring.

"I'll help you if I can," John answered in a milder tone, wondering a little. "What do you wish?"

"Shawcross is my name, sir—James Shawcross, lieutenant in the Maryland battalion," the man repeated, stepping closer to John and wavering as he walked although he had no smell of drink about him. "I suffer from an indisposition, a sickness of long standing. Dr. Redman of Philadelphia has treated me for it. 'Tis a dry retching, very painful, most undignified in an officer—"

"Now burn me!" John burst out. "Have you come to complain of a colic?"

"My concern is not for myself," Shawcross went on, his vacant look and the constant trembling of his hands, as John now observed them, at odds with the soft persistence of his voice. "My men will take notice of it. They'll misconceive my trouble."

"Well, then?"

"You must send me to Jersey."

"Discharge you on a day of battle!"

"I'll hold you blameless, sir. I'll report the matter to the commanding general. He'll understand my scruple."

"He'll understand that you're sick with fear—" John broke off his speech, instantly regretting the brutal words which his own anxieties had prompted. "Be advised by me," he continued more calmly, "and say no more. The fort is invested. With leave or without it, you cannot get clear of this place."

Shawcross began to shake, his head nodding up and down in a parody of assent.

"Send me away," he whispered hoarsely. "You can do it." And then in a shout: "For the love of God, let me go!"

John seized him by the shoulders and held him fast. He offered no resistance.

"Look here at me!" John ordered. "Look at my mates! Don't you think we're as frighted as you? Call up your pride, man. You'll soon grow used to this evil business—aye, and laugh at it in time."

"You weren't there. You weren't by the Brooklyn road. I didn't see you there." Shawcross clutched suddenly at John's arm, gripping so hard that it hurt. He looked full in John's face, yet his pale eyes seemed to gaze through John and beyond him. "They couldn't budge us. Not a foot, though they played all morning on us with shell and round-shot. That was when the first ones died. How could you know what it was like?" The man's voice rose. "You weren't there; I'll make oath to that. Listen, then! Stirling rode up to us at eleven o'clock. 'Quit yourselves like men,' he told us. 'We're all lost unless you stop them.' He'd watched them come round in the rear, d'you see, on our line of retreat—seen them making for the road by the creek and the house up above it. It was built of stone, that house; it had walls as thick as a church. Major Gist knew what he meant. We faced left and charged but they'd lodged in the house by the time we reached it. We ran right up to the windows —five times we ran up, and the grape and canister beating on us like hail. I left Ned Albright by the wall, all over blood like a stuck pig. He was one of my farmers, was Ned; he'd only come to the war because of me. Then the grenadiers took us in flank and we broke for the swamp—"

A single gun spoke from the southward, a heavy sound like the thump of a maul upon wood. Immediately after, a fury of fire arose all around the compass, the reports crowding on one another, echoing off the

hills and merging in a single enormous uproar. Shawcross stood still a moment longer, mouthing speech
without words. Then he clapped both hands in agony
over his ears and ran off, veering crazily among the
hastily forming files.

The sky was bright now. Dust rose in clouds under
scuffling feet as the garrison scrambled to the alarm
posts. Colonel Magaw hurried out from the headquarters tent, belting on his sword as he came. Followed
close by three of his aides, he ran down the parade and
left the fort by the north gate.

No time now to fret over one poor craven, thought
John, yet the fellow was a coward with a difference.
Something more than fear had unmanned him. Men did
curious things in war and curious inspirations possessed
them. Two nights before, as the supper fires were
lighted, a sergeant of Atlee's old regiment had risen suddenly and gone snivelling from company to company,
begging to know if he'd injured anyone and if he were
forgiven for it. Some of the soldiers had turned from
him in silence; others had given him a rough comfort; a
few had mocked him.

The guns had been busy for more than three hours.
Looking eastward from the parapet, John saw the sun
standing pale and cold over the thick woods by the
Harlem and the smoke of the cannonade eddying up
and hanging cloud-like about the heights beyond that
river. Below him, a puff of wind sent the dead leaves
whirling along the base of the earthen wall. A haze still
veiled the shore, not two miles off, where the enemy
must be waiting. Although he could not see them, he

imagined the red battalions there, steady in ranks for the crossing. Smoke hung in the southward too, and the thump of cannon was louder from that quarter. The talk of the riflemen who stood beside him sounded lonely and small.

Doubtless there were many wounded in the lines, yet none had been brought to the fort as yet. Round-shot need not be deadly against a well-sited position, he told himself; at Boston the men had scorned it. But bombshells with their fiery flare and a concussion that tore men to bits were another matter. The bayonet, too! Militiamen feared the bayonet. The defenders of the outposts would be crouching in shallow trenches or in the brushwood cover, muttering oaths and stale obscenities to keep their courage up, awaiting action with the dumb fortitude of men who sense that the account is cast against them and still hope. He put the thought from his mind, for he could not afford to think of soldiers as faces, voices, names. They were only bones and flesh, tendons, muscles, veins; they were stricken and broken things which he must mend.

Five horsemen came up the Kingsbridge road at a gallop, halted at a sentry's challenge, and then climbed the stony path to the fort at a walking pace. As they passed beneath him, John recognized Magaw and his aides; the fifth man was a stranger. Whence had they come? What had they learned? No matter, John thought, feeling shame at the anxiety that had seized on him. It was not his concern how the battle should be fought.

Stamping their feet and shifting about for warmth, the garrison companies waited for what would come.

The men were silent for the most part and looked worn-out in the full light of morning. Hairy of face and motley in dress, they carried weapons of every style and age—muskets from the British store-ships captured off Boston, flintlocks, and fowling pieces. Their coats and breeches were ragged patchwork, filthy with months of entrenching labor and field service. Many wore woollen scarves drawn over their ears and knotted beneath their chins; others had padded out their coats or hunting-shirts with extra stockings and lengths of shoddy cloth. Half-trained, hungry, undisciplined, how could they hope for victory?

The waiting was the worst of war as John had observed it. Action was a release, he thought, a brief renewal of importance, a rouse of the spirit despite the danger. And then he wondered without reason where Shawcross had fled to, in what place the man had hidden himself like a wounded beast.

He returned to the hospital. Mason, the mate, lay dozing; Gillespie was crouched beside the steaming caldron, whistling a hymn-tune and poking at the fire. Their easiness rasped on John's nerves.

"Up, you lubbers!" he ordered. "Find something useful to do!"

Hardly had he spoken when the clamor of cannon ceased. All along the walls, the guards and the idle gunners were shouting and waving their arms. Cries of command rang out; the alarm drums were beat. From the east, and from the south also, musketry clattered on the frosty air. Volleys first; then a diminishing, ragged popping; then volleys again.

A rifleman sprang down from the firestep and ran to-

ward the headquarters tent. John caught him by the
arm as he passed the hospital hut, questioning him.

"They're making for Sherman's Creek," the man replied. "They've started over the Harlem." Great guns
opened fire at the north, sounding quite near at hand.
"Them's ours," he cried, jerking his arm free, "from up
over Kingsbridge. The Germans must be stirring too—"

The waiting was at an end.

He was no more than twenty but his wan face and the
hollows under his cheekbones gave him an unnatural
look of age. His dirty linen hunting-shirt was crimsoned
and stiff with blood. A ball had traversed his upper right
arm; it had passed through and out, as John satisfied
himself with a probe. The rifleman winced, setting his
teeth against a cry.

"Too many of 'em," he muttered. "They dug us out
like we was moles."

"Where did you stand?"

"In the second line." He nodded southward. "We
won't hold there for long. Light infantry was afore us
and Scotchmen on the left." He snatched at the mug
which Gillespie held out to him and swigged off the rum
at a gulp.

The militia stood fast at Laurel Hill. One of the earli-
est wounded had said so, had assured John that all went
well. An hour ago? Or three? He had lost count of time.
Too many maimed men had come in since, stumbling
through the gates on their own legs or borne to the hospital by stragglers. Once, as he had looked up from his
labors, he had seen Colonel Magaw pacing about—head
hanging forward and hands clasped tight behind his

back. A man much troubled, a man most unlike the bold defier of Howe.

John's fingers were stiff with cold and strain; it was not good, even for the butcher's work he had to do. A dozen men and more were awaiting treatment, some standing in mute pain, others groaning on the straw. Outside the hut, Mason was watching over those whose wounds had already been dressed. In a row in the bright cold, wrapped in what rags of cover the mates could beg from sound men, they kept up a piercing chorus of cries and complaints. Opposite them, in a second row, lay the first to die under the knife.

The fire of enemy cannon resumed. It was a continuous bass roar with no intervals and the volleys of musketry rang out over it like distinct notes of a sullen music. The garrison companies stirred nervously in ranks. All ignorant of what was happening, they had used up their stock of patience and grew unruly.

Two soldiers hoisted a third up on to the amputating table. The wounded man's left foot was a shapeless mass; a round shot had crushed it. His head lolled to one side and he babbled, for his friends had filled him with rum to ease him. As John began to saw his leg off short of the knee, he screamed—a dreadful neighing sound. Then he lay limp and insensible. When the work was done, Gillespie twisted a cord tight around the spouting stump and John laid the cautery to it. The table was slick with blood. Gillespie wiped it with a handful of straw.

No hope for the next man; a ball had entered his belly and burst him. Then a bayonet thrust through a thigh, very neat and deep.

John labored like a man in a fever. The din had become intolerable; his head throbbed with it. And now Gillespie was shouting something in his ear, pointing to the caldron.

"There's no more water."

"Send Mason to fetch some."

John stood back from the table, shuddering. The hurt in his head had induced a kind of vertigo; he had almost fallen. Fixing his gaze on the ground and turning very slowly, he walked with faltering steps to the front of the hut and stood there, clutching at a wooden post for support. When his tremors lessened and he dared raise his eyes, the sight before him seemed a vision of delirium.

The gate at the north stood wide. Through it, disordering and dismaying all in their path, a horde of militamen rioted in and ran heedless everywhere; they were blind with panic and howling like the lost. The standing companies of the garrison were broken asunder into struggling, cursing bands of frightened men. Disregarded, thrust aside in the confusion, the officers flailed about them with the flats of their swords. Cannon on the northeast bastion opened, crash upon crash.

A sturdy figure came shouldering through the melée and over to the hospital. It was James McHenry from Laurel Hill, clutching his bag of instruments in bloody hands.

"All's over with us on the hill," he cried to John. "The men did their best. They stood up to the Guards like heroes 'til Colonel Baxter fell."

"Are the British at hand?"

"They've halted below in the woods. I'd sent you all my wounded, so I had no mind to stay and be taken—" He ended his speech abruptly, staring hard at John.

"Damme, man, you're a ghost," he went on, speaking with a real concern. "You're overtasked. You must rest."

John tarried at the entrance to the hut, recovering his wits a little in the bite of the air and with sight of the wide, cold sky. Childlike, he wondered what was happening beyond the walls; what lurked outside in the woods. The great guns were silent now, but the wounded shouted and wailed. Like a sleepwalker, he watched the tumult slowly subside; watched the garrison troops and the routed militia form ranks again; watched Mason return with water, driving a line of laden soldiers before him.

"No blankets? Aye. Then they must die, a many of them." McHenry looked down at the wounded with a face of granite. "They'll die for want of a length of wool."

The rasping, angry voice fell silent. Outside, a new clamor had arisen to the southward. It drew closer, closer, and now it was just below the wall—a scurry and crying, like sheep in alarm and flight. McHenry shouted something but his words were lost in a rending crash. The cannoneers on the south wall fired, ran their guns in, swabbed and loaded and fired again; they worked swiftly and intently, with the ordered movements of a set of dancers. The riflemen showered down shot, leaning out over the parapet to aim. Reserve companies raced past, stumbling over one another, mounting to the firesteps.

The north gate swung inward again. By hundreds, and foul with dirt and powder-stain, a second rout of fugitives stormed through it. They kept a better order than the rout from Laurel Hill and the ranks stood firm to receive them, yet the crowding was fearsome. The open ground of Fort Washington teemed with men.

A grey-faced captain of the 4th Pennsylvania regiment was first of the newcomers at the hospital. He was only lightly hurt but full of anger at his wound. Lord Percy's horse-soldiers and the wild Highlanders had pressed the pursuit from the southern lines almost up to the fort.

"Club yer muskets agin 'em when yer powder's spent. That's what the Cunnel told us. Let him try it hisself, I says. Let's see how he'll fare—"

While he dressed the man's wound, John asked what had chanced with Hearn.

"The surgeon, d'ye mean? The sharp-nosed man with the cough? He's dead. Sabered as we left the lines. They meant for us all to die, I tell you. Our own people who put us there. They meant for us to die."

The enemy made no assault from the south. The cannonade dwindled and ceased. Except for a distant and fitful crackle of rifle-fire, the burden of noise was human for a little while—a restless scuffling of feet, the cries of the wounded, the bustle of the powder carriers, a harsh contention of voices from the nearby headquarters tent.

Volleys of musketry echoed suddenly from the north, almost instant in succession, a long roll of menace. John felt his stomach turn. His hands trembled and he looked down at them with vague reproach, thinking that he must not trust them with the knife.

Colonel Magaw hurried forth from his tent. Pausing by the row of wounded, he turned a furious face on the young, spruce officer who had followed him.

"No," he cried. "No! It's not possible."

"Only 'til dusk," the young man urged, raising his voice to be heard above the volleys. "We'll bring you off in boats."

"Boats! While British warships command the river? They must all be mad at headquarters. Whose counsel was this?"

"I've given you the General's order, sir."

"Look about you!" The Colonel flung out his arms. "Would you hold men here in this slaughter-pen? When Howe moves his cannon up close, he'll use plunging fire. 'Tis hopeless, hopeless, hopeless. It was so from the outset."

"He daren't mount an assault," said the young man, confidently. "You could Bunker Hill him."

Magaw stood quiet, grinding his fist into the palm of his other hand.

"Go back to Fort Lee," he said at last. "The Germans are close by the cove but you still have a chance. Tell the General that I promise nothing."

The young officer ran off, forcing his way through the press of men to the west wall.

"No bandages," McHenry called to John. "I've searched in the stores. No lint even!"

The guns along the north parapet spoke with one great voice; the cannon smoke rolled back over the fort in an acrid cloud. Again the guns were fired, and again, while the musketry volleys stuttered into silence. Then, from the near distance, shouting. A hoarse cheer, and again a cheer. The men in ranks were coughing in the smoke.

Defeat flooded in through the gate for the third time, a scurry of Marylanders in red and brown-shirted Virginia riflemen. Many sought refuge among the garrison companies but as many more clambered up on the wall and joined in the fusillade against their pursuers.

Four artillerymen bore a bloodied figure on a litter into the hospital.

"Look you here, Frayne!" exclaimed McHenry. "A woman—and she's sliced and hacked like mutton!"

"Corbin's wife, she is," spoke up one of the bearers. "She wouldna gae off wi' the rest of the women, poor soul. And she sairved her husband's gun when he fell."

"Them Germans is deevils," another said. "They clumb up the rocks out there like our fire was rain in their faces. 'Twas an awful thing when they came at us with the steel. They'd a man to lead them though, by God! He tore our breastwork down with his own bare hands."

The sound of small-arms fell away, swelled, and fell away again in an unsteady, dying pulse. The cannon were dumb. Swarming shoulder to shoulder in the fort, the men brawled amongst themselves, striking out with fists, bewildered, mutinous. Cadwalader, who had commanded in the southern lines, ran about the parade with Magaw, pleading that they stand like soldiers.

"Lead us out there then," the rankers shouted. "We'll make the bloody-backs run—and the Germans too." Cadwalader shook his head. He tried to speak but they smothered his voice with their angry noise.

John labored alongside Mason over the row of

wounded. Some had already died and their staring eyes filled him with horror. These maimed and dead made a mock of their comrades' brag. The truth of war was here.

The end came at a little after midday. All firing ceased of a sudden.

Surprised by quiet, John looked up from his work. He saw McHenry gazing all agape, and the mates also, and on the wall the riflemen leaning down and calling something to their nearest fellows. Swiftly, the news passed from mouth to mouth in a swell of sound.

"What are they saying?" McHenry cried, tugging at John's arm. "Can you hear it?"

Colonel Magaw brushed past them, and Cadwalader. The commandant disappeared within his tent and Cadwalader took up post just outside it, flanked by two captains. His face was twitching; he licked his lips. The now docile troops were ordered and hustled about so as to leave a path open down the length of the parade. John could hear from beyond the walls the thin but confident ruffle of a drum.

The north gate was opened, men straining to draw it back. Led by a guide in a hunting-shirt, a blindfolded drummer entered; behind them walked a lanky officer, also blindfolded, who carried a musket to which a white cloth was fastened. In dark blue coat and buff breeches, his high leather boots powdered with dust, he followed the guide and the drummer down between the silent ranks until they halted before Cadwalader.

"Hohenstein, captain in the regiment of Rall," the bluecoat announced in excellent English, taking off his hat and bowing. "Do I stand before the commander of this place?"

"I speak for him," Cadwalader replied.

"The drummer and I were fired upon just now," the German remarked. "All the way, sir, as we crossed the cleared ground to the *glacis*. It is not polite, that. It is not the custom of war."

"I deplore the action, captain."

"You are rebellious subjects, not soldiers, so I make allowance for it," the German went on. "We shall say no more of it. And now to my business, sir. You are invested on all sides. Your situation is bad, and it will be worse when we bring our cannon to play. I am instructed, therefore, to demand your immediate surrender. You must march out with all your men and you must lay down your arms before General von Knyphausen. You must make known and yield up all public property and materials of war in your possession. Your personal property you may keep, and so may your men. Finally, you must hoist a white flag at once to signal the end of fighting."

"Colonel Magaw will need time to consider your terms."

"There is a question of honor here," said Magaw. He had come out from the tent while the German was speaking and although he looked haggard and anxious he tried to speak with a note of confidence. "The terms are hard and my reponsibility is great."

"My own orders are precise," Hohenstein replied. "I cannot exceed them."

"Surely you can listen to a counter-proposal."

"My orders forbid it." Hohenstein bowed again, as if

to soften the harshness of his speech. "I can only suggest that you come with me to my general. He waits outside, no more than two hundred paces from the gate. You can make your proposals to him."

"You are most obliging," answered Magaw, bowing in his turn. "I shall take your safe-conduct and go to your general."

Magaw returned from his mission some twenty minutes later. As he walked in at the gate, a hush lay over the fort like the stillness in a house of mourning. His dejected look and air were warrant enough of his failure but the rank-and-file were not wholly persuaded of it until he mounted a firestep and began to recite the terms of capitulation to them. Then they burst out in a great cry of protest, ranting, cursing and dashing their firearms against the ground. Only the wounded were passive, not caring.

"He's sold us," McHenry shouted. "He should hang for this."

John observed with wonder that Gillespie was weeping. Big tears were coursing down the fellow's hard, shrewd face as he fumbled with a loosened bandage. He himself felt only hunger now, an animal emptiness, and the sting of the cold.

CHAPTER FOUR

THE PRISONERS were mustered in a long meadow at the foot of the heights they had hoped to defend. Listless and hungry, they stared out at the stir of enemy traffic along the Kingsbridge road. Hessian soldiers, relieved of duty, preyed on them like kites, snatching away their hats and blanket-rolls, stripping off their coats, and pulling off their shoes to search for currency or coins. The bluecoats who guarded them made no effort to protect them.

John Frayne stood amid an unkempt throng of Pennsylvania militiamen near the southern extremity of the meadow and just opposite the Blue Bell tavern which the British had taken for a temporary headquarters. No one had heeded his protests that he was a surgeon and an officer. The Hessians who occupied the hospital after the surrender had been in no mood for parleys, even had they spoken English. Their captain had indicated by signs that McHenry and the mates should continue the work with the wounded; his men had thrust John by main force into the general mass of prisoners.

It was only late afternoon, yet it seemed an age since

the defeated Americans had marched out of the fort between a double line of the regiments of Lossberg and Rall. The German general, his uniform all muddied and rent after his exertions at the head of the storming column, had reviewed the captives as they laid down their arms; his face had been as empty of feeling as the face of an antique warrior carved in stone.

Overspent, shivering in the chill wind, John could not turn his mind from the thought of betrayal. Had Hearn been right in his surmise? All that had happened since morning seemed to confirm it. A prudent general would have withdrawn the garrison earlier, even as Washington had offered to do too late. Or was that offer a part of the base design of Congress, meant only to deceive? It were unforgivable if the wounded and the dead, these scarecrows among whom he stood in the meadow—aye, and Magaw and Cadwalader too—had been sacrificed for a show. And a sorry and useless show, in the event! Fort Washington had been no Thermopylae; no legend of heroes would spring from its wasting and fall.

When a suet-faced bluecoat made off with his pocketbook and money, John offered no resistance. It appeared a minor grievance after such a day of discontents.

A company of British soldiers, headed by a sullen-looking officer on horseback, came up the road from the south and halted by the tavern. Hardly had they done so, when a commotion began among the prisoners. One of the militiamen seized a looting German by the throat. As the nearest of the guards rushed up with presented bayonets, the American's comrades stood about him to protect him. On the instant, the British officer spurred over, reared his horse above the combatants, and laid the small whip which he carried on guards and prisoners alike.

"Is this how you keep your watch?" he shouted to the captain of the guard. " 'Tis death to plunder. The terms of surrender forbid it."

"These are rebels and dogs," the German answered angrily.

"They are indeed—but what's writ in the treaty is writ, and by your own general too. No matter," the Englishman went on, "for I've orders here to relieve you of the rogues." And he pulled out a paper from a pocket of his coat.

The Germans drew off and the British soldiers set about ranging the prisoners in line of march.

"Away with ye!" scoffed the young lieutenant to whom John renewed his protest that he was a surgeon of the hospital. "Ye're all colonels by your own account. Mark this noisy fellow, sergeant! If he lags on the march, beat him."

The prisoners shambled forward on to the road and trudged off southward, shepherded on either flank by silent, indifferent, redcoat rankers. The mounted officer, sitting easy in the saddle, rode alongside the toiling column, now moving up to its head, now dropping back, his eye alert for the least breach of discipline. He had not long to wait for one. Of a sudden, a tall man ran out from his place in line, caught hold of the horseman's stirrup, and clung to it. Heedless of the blows and shouts of the guards, the oaths of the officer, or the stamp of the startled horse's hooves, he tightened his grip on the stirrup, crying out in a high desperate voice that John remembered well: "I must go free. I shall die. I shall die."

It was the fellow who had come that morning to beg a leave, the malingerer. Shawcross was his name. The column plodded on. The pleading voice lessened with distance and was still.

The long line halted near Colonel Morris's fine house on the hill overlooking Harlem River. Before the battle at the White Plains, the American army had kept headquarters there; now the barns and outbuildings were a bank of deposit for prisoners, those taken in the field as well as the captured garrison of Fort Washington. John was confined in a cattle shed with some eighty other men. The air soon became foul after the single door was closed and more than an hour passed before it was unbarred to permit a few buckets of water to be handed in. The opening of the door freshened the air in the shed yet this small mercy was more than offset by the presence of a number of British light infantry officers who peered in at the prisoners and taunted them. "We've cub foxes in plenty here," said one. " 'Tis pity that Washington is got to his earth in Jersey. Look you here, corporal of the guard! These rebels crowd too close to the entry. Teach 'em manners with your musket butt."

The watch was changed just before dusk and a gray-haired captain of the 27th Regiment succeeded to command. He had a dour look and he limped slightly as from an old wound but his humor was kindly. He made an immediate inspection of the teeming barns and sheds, provided a sufficient supply of water, and ordered away all persons who were not in fact on guard duty.

When he entered the place where John was confined, he expressed his regret that he had no rations for the prisoners. He and his men were in a like plight, he said. Let them be patient until morning. All would be fed.

The cold stung him and hunger gnawed him but John was soon in a heavy sleep.

At dawn the prisoners were roused and mustered in a line outside the shed. The captain was as good as his word. The fare provided was bully-beef and bread, coarse food but in plenty, and John and his comrades ate ravenously of it. As soon as they had finished, the guards formed them in column of fours and took up positions flanking them. It was the Sabbath, as John recalled, but there was no observance of the day.

"Mind the step, hold your heads high, and do yourselves credit," the elderly captain called out from his place at the head of the column. "Ye still can look soldier-like, even though ye be captivated." With that, he swung about and led them off down the road, stepping brisk and proud to the tap of the drum for all that his gait was halt.

After they entered the enemy's lines at Harlem, they were taken eastward to a pasture where they stood a long time. Other parties of prisoners were brought in to join them there, and at last the whole body of Americans was strung out in column between files of redcoats for a triumphal progress into the city of New York.

They tramped at a steady pace for an hour and more past open fields and deserted country-houses. Just before they came to the junction of the road from Kingsbridge with the Bowery lane, near where a tree-lined path turned off to the Stuyvesant houses by the river, they

were given an inkling of what they must expect as captives. A throng of Tory civilians, Negroes, and soldiers'
bawds had come out thus far from town to greet them
with jeers and curses. The poor drabs were the most
vehement in their loyal sentiments, clawing at the
guards in their zeal to attack the prisoners and returning from each repulse with added fury. These vicious
scoundrels were joined by others of their kind as they
followed the marchers down to the city's northern limits, so that the redcoats were hard put to keep them at a
distance.

The head of the line was brought to a halt near a
tavern surrounded by empty cattle pens and the prisoners were suffered to stand at ease. Water was given them,
but no food. The attending mob was held at bay by the
menaces of the guard but it could not be silenced.

"Yankee rebels, ye're a-goin' to the gallows, a-goin' to
the gallows, a-goin' to the gallows—"

Beyond the tavern, the great sails of a windmill
turned slowly against a clouding western sky. The
streets that extended to right and to left of the Bowery
lane were unimproved for the most part on the side
where the tavern stood but they were built up on the
eastward to a depth of several blocks or squares with
wooden shacks and small, mean houses of brick. To the
south and west, the public slaughter-house stood beside
the Collect or fresh-water pond, whence a vacant tract of
marshy land ran all the way to the Hudson. Below the
pond lay the dusty common—the Fields, as the Yorkers
called it—with its rows of barracks, the gray stone bulk
of the Debtors' Gaol, and the still unfinished Bridewell.

St. Paul's Church at the southern extremity of the common was one of several churches which loomed up over the mass of less distinguished structures, and adjoining St. Paul's on a gentle rise to the north was the King's College building, until lately the general hospital of the army of America. Nearer at hand, John observed yet other landmarks which had become familiar during his walks about the city during the previous spring and summer—the redoubts and entrenchments dug for the city's defense, the Bayard house on a hill overlooking the Collect, and the noble house and gardens far to the east at Mount Pitt where Thomas Jones, a justice of the Province, had kept great state in happier times.

John had been afoot since dawn and had not eaten since that time but the hopeless humor which the battle and its sequel had inspired no longer oppressed him. While his neighbors stood dumpish and silent, or muttered glumly to one another, he turned his whole mind to his own situation and what he could do to improve it.

He would seek a parole, first of all. The British Provost would never so favor a common soldier, therefore he must identify himself and assert his proper degree before some responsible official. Once he was free on parole, he would have leisure for thought—and this he craved beyond all else. If, as it now appeared, the defenders of Fort Washington had been sacrificed for a political gambit, the great adventure for all men's rights had come to a sorry end. Yet he could not be certain that this was the fact. He must think well on it, and on what his own future role must be. George Washington had seemed a wise and worthy leader at Boston. What must be thought of him now, after his successive defeats around New York and his sacrifice of the fort? Had he failed in judgment, or had he indeed sunk to be a creature of intriguing politicians? And what of the Congress itself? The Virginians were all-powerful in its councils, and they were lords of vast acres, masters of slaves, Could anything but vanity and self-seeking be expected of such men? Could they be trusted to uphold the rights of all men in an independent America?

He would go home to Wendham and search out the answers to his questions in retirement. His return would occasion no surprise, he thought with a sour smile. During his last visit home, the town had been brisk with sometime militiamen and patriots—all busy, all thriving —whose zeal for liberty had cooled after a few weeks' service before Boston. They could ill afford to criticize him. His coming would pleasure his mother too; it would exercise her gift for irony. "Will you throw your life away for a whim?" she had asked him when he first went off to the army. Here was another question to be answered.

If the British refused his parole and imprisoned him, he would have to contrive an escape. In his present resolute mood, he was confident of success. Once at large in New York, who could say if he were Whig or Tory? He need only throw away the cockade from his hat to be anonymous in this turbulent city. He had come to know it well since he first stepped ashore at the wharf near Whitehall seven months ago, and now he recognized with the wisdom of an empty belly and a sad heart that the first seeds of his disillusion had been sown there.

After Boston had been taken in March, the army of America had moved southward to foil an expected descent of the enemy upon New York. John had marched with the 12th Regiment of the line, Colonel Moses Little commanding, as far as New London in Connecticut, whence they had completed their passage by ship down Long Island Sound. The regiment had disembarked on the 16th of April in bright weather and in high health and spirits, but a fatality had enveloped the army almost immediately.

The city of New York proper was contained within an ambit of about a mile square at the tip of the island of Manhattan. It had been a lively, pleasant place, doubtless, in time of peace, but with its narrow streets barricaded and the shade trees all cut down for fortification and firewood, New York appeared grim and disheartening and John envied his comrades who had gone to duty in the open country on Long Island.

The Broadway, which ran northwards from the crumbling fort at the city's southern extremity, was the principal street for residence; the rising ground on the west side, from the fort to just below Trinity Church, was the genteelest part. On the north and west, St. Paul's Church and the College building nearby it marked the limits of the city; beyond the College was open land, criss-crossed with newly dug entrenchments. Commerce was carried on to the eastward, where a warren of wharves and quays was linked to Queen Street, the chief thoroughfare in that quarter, by strait and twisting alleys and by tidal waterways known as slips. Queen Street was lined with ware-rooms and counting-houses in whose upper stories the merchants of the city had dwelt within comfortable reach of their wealth and merchandise. Hanover Square abutted on Queen Street and was a handsome place with shops of a particular elegance. Yet all the glories of this commercial Babylon had departed with war and the death of trade. The wharves and the slips were empty, the ware-rooms and shops were barren of goods. Many of the more considerable men of business had barred their doors or had fled to the country.

John was quartered with five officers of the staff in a house on Nassau Street near the Middle Dutch Church. The householder had gone off to safety in Jersey, taking all his furniture with him, and the new occupants slept in their blankets on the bare floor. John and his fellows made a jest of their own discomfort but the evidence of confusion which was everywhere apparent was no laughing matter to them or to any thinking man.

The move from Boston had been executed in haste and without preparation; the defenders of New York were less an army than an enthusiastic, wasteful, undisciplined mob. Along the Broadway, and up and down the cross streets and the waterfront ways, lounged thousands of men with mouths agape and naught to do— militiamen and Continental regulars, men in blue broadcloth and in brown butternut, frontiersmen in hunting-shirts and trim, redcoated Marylanders, Yorkers and Yankees, Pennsylvanians and Virginians. Their unvaried diet of salt meat and sea-bread was well contrived to sicken even the hardiest of them, and the mingling of men from all the colonies scattered the local contagions of each section broadcast through the army. Idleness and indiscipline encouraged venery, so that the foxy jades and strumpets who inhabited the "holy ground" above Trinity Church and who flaunted along Robinson Street at the very gate of the general hospital were in a roaring way of trade. Drunken, reeling men and women, fighting and screaming murder, were daily taken up by the guard and hurried off by dozens to the Provost.

The city was soon a pest-hole. Sick men lay close against one another in the rooms and corridors of the King's College building and in sundry warehouses and abandoned dwellings which were commandeered for hospital use. The chief cause of the crowding was a dearth of men to serve as nurses or waiters on the sick. None of the common soldiers would volunteer for the duty and those who were ordered to perform it took the first opportunity to desert. The crowding and the noxious airs made any morbid sickness equivalent to death and the sound of funeral music was heard each day until a general order forbade its use.

At festering New York, just as before Boston, John Morgan had struggled to impose order on the medical service. As active with his pen as he was in the sick-rooms, the director of the hospital denounced the medical committee of Congress for its failure to provide supplies, the commissaries for purveying unwholesome food, and the camp-masters for neglecting to dig latrines. Small thanks he had for his efforts, and little to show. Dysentery soon became a general contagion in the city. Men's lives drained away through their own bowels and nothing availed to cure the distemper, not purging nor opium nor bleeding. A bilious putrid fever raged as well and was equally baffling to the physicians. Some of them held that it was caused by the prevalent humid weather. Morgan scoffed at this opinion, yet the heat and dampness were indeed exceptional. The land grew parched; the grass browned and failed. Men who had followed the sea said that this was no common summer weather; it was more like the climate of tropic ports where death lay hid in the low, white fogs and a prudent captain secured all his portholes at night.

Such was the state of health in the army on the 25th of June when the first of more than four hundred British sail appeared off Sandy Hook. Warships and transports continued to make harbor during the weeks that followed until a vast fleet rode at anchor in the bay of New York and a superb body of troops under Sir William Howe had been landed on Staten Island. By mid-August, Sir William was ready to move against the city. On August 22nd, he came ashore in force at Gravesend on Long Island.

John Frayne went at once from the hospital to his alarm post at Fort Greene, a star-shaped work on a hill at about the center of the semi-circle of forts, entrenchments and outworks which had been built with much labor around the village of Brooklyn. These lines, as they were called, defended the shortest approach by water to the island of Manhattan and were drawn from the Gowanus marshes on the west to the Wallabout bay on the east. Directly before the lines, at about two miles' distance across level country, rose the heights of Gowanus—a range of low, wooded hills separating Brooklyn from Flatbush and other smaller hamlets in the wide plain that sloped southward to the ocean. The heights were traversed by four passes, and as it was expected that the enemy's thrust from Gravesend would come through one or several of them, they were all manned and fortified.

John had learned that Ben Ripley and Abijah Flagg, his sometime comrades of the Wendham minuteman company, were with Hitchcock's regiment at the Flatbush pass and he purposed to visit them. But this was not to be. On the 27th of August, the British and their German auxiliaries attacked and overcame the defenders at three of the passes, took a great number of prisoners, and laid siege to the Brooklyn lines. Three days later, the American garrison abandoned the lines and escaped in boats to Manhattan.

The retreat was made in haste, by night, and under cover of rain and fog, so that the boatmen took little trouble with the wounded and sick. John and his fellow surgeons removed these unfortunates to the hospital from the wharves and other unsuitable places where they had been lodged, but almost immediately after, by order of General Greene, many of them were allowed to wander off through Jersey in the care of regimental surgeons. The population of the hospital was greatly reduced thereby but the contagions of camp fever and dysentery were spread wherever the sick were harbored.

As a descent of the enemy on the island of Manhattan was certain, the main body of the army of America had been withdrawn from the city and was assembled in a posture of observation near Kingsbridge and on the heights above Harlem. All day and all night, in stifling heat, the magazines of military stores in the city were emptied and their contents freighted to the north. Through the open windows of the King's College build-

ing, there came a continuous noise from across the
Common—the rumble of gun carriages, powder carts
and provision wagons; the squeal of axles overladen
with tents, baggage, and camp gear of every kind; the
crack of whips and the crackle of oaths as the teamsters
flogged their weary animals up the Kingsbridge road.

With so much care given the stores, John thought, a
little might have been spared for the wounded, yet he
had received no word of what he must do with them.
Morgan had gone to seek a proper site for a new general
hospital in nearby Jersey and John had heard nothing
from him since his departure. Detachments from General Putnam's division and from Knox's artillery were
still in the city and four brigades were on patrol along
the lower shores of the Hudson and East rivers, but the
removal of wounded was not their business.

Early in the morning of September 15th, a cannonade
shook the hospital to its foundations. John had only to
look out the broken window nearest him to see four
men-of-war standing off in the Hudson and engaging the
American batteries along both sides of the river. By nine
o'clock, the ships had passed by to the north and the
Sabbath was quiet again.

Two hours later, a discharge of cannon began on the
eastern side of the island, so great in volume and in-
cessant that it seemed close at hand. The sick men were
nervous and fretful at first, especially the many with
feverish chest complaints, but John and his helpers pre-
served their own poise of mind and the patients became
calmer.

The cannon fire ceased at about one in the afternoon.
It was succeeded by a distant noise of musketry and then

by a silence at the eastward, more alarming than the previous horrid din. After an anxious hour of waiting, a noise of running feet was heard outside and a captain of artillery put his head in at the door.

"The British are ashore at Kip's Bay," he cried. "The city's lost. Remove your wounded to Harlem."

"How?"

"By the side roads along the Hudson. The main road's been cut."

As this seemed the only order that he was likely to receive, John bade the mates and waiters prepare the sick for travel. Those who could walk must do so; the others would be carried on improvised stretchers. A dozen commissary wagons should be enough for transport, and Morgan's name must be his warrant to impress them and their drivers.

When he ran up the path to Broadway and looked across the common to where the Kingsbridge road branched off at the right, his confidence ebbed. He could see only panic and a confusion of jettisoned stores and baggage. The Commissary's men were knocking out the heads of flour barrels and spilling the contents in the dirt; over by the Bridewell, a great heap of canvas was going up in smoke. Drovers were urging herds of lowing and stumbling livestock along the road out of the city. The few wagons in view were cram-full of men in flight who would stop for no one. Less fortunate soldiers of the city garrison were running away on foot. It was thunder-gust weather, intolerably hot and close.

John halted a militia sergeant and begged his help in conscripting stretcher bearers, but the fellow would have none of it.

"The men won't listen to me," he shouted. "They've no more mind to wait and be took than I have. Don't you hear that bicker of muskets over yonder? That there's the British!"

As he hastened back to the hospital, John noted with surprise that the walking wounded were moving in a ragged line down the path to the riverside. He had quickened his pace to a run and had shouted to them to halt before he caught sight of the small, gaunt, modish figure overseeing the removal. It was John Morgan, returned in the nick of time.

"You look out of patience," the director remarked as John approached him. "They told me that you were off seeking transport and help. You found neither, of course. All common men are selfish swine, my dear Frayne—just as all statesmen are vain and all soldiers vainglorious. I was at Harlem when the attack began, and as I've learned not to look for foresight among military gentlemen, I pressed a fair number of boats on my own responsibility. They wait below in the cove. I'll see the sick men safe aboard, and do you be good enough to gather and load our supplies. If they be lost, God knows where we'll get more."

The boats were all clear save one by the time the first redcoated skirmishers appeared on the College plot and began to move with great caution against the vacant building. The medicines had been saved but a great part of the lint, blankets, and cloth for bandages still cluttered the sandy beach and had to be abandoned. While John and the men who had been helping him were clambering into the last boat, the skirmishers observed them and started down the path to the cove. The boatmen laid to their oars; the boat shot out into the stream. A few musket balls, indifferently aimed and harmless, spattered in the water astern. Escaping notice by the warships on station up river, the boats all came safe ashore above Harlem and within the American lines.

The general hospital was formally established in Jersey a few days later, and John served there until he was ordered to Fort Washington.

The wind had dropped off to nothing; beyond the tavern, the sails of the windmill hung motionless against the now fully overcast sky. John rubbed his hands together and stamped his tingling feet. Either it had grown colder or he was more aware of the cold. How long had he day-dreamed? A half-hour? Perhaps longer. All around him the prisoners stood silent, each man lost in his own misery. The onlookers were silent too. Many of the jeering mob had gone off about their own concerns but a fixed malevolence persisted in the oafish countenances of those who remained.

A group of officers rode up and the redcoat guards sprang to attention. Orders passed down the line of command and the prisoners were reassembled four afront in companies of a hundred. John's company was marched at a rapid pace across a corner of the Common and by way of William Street to the North Dutch Church; it was brought to a halt in front of the principal door.

The decent edifice had suffered a sad change since John had last seen it. A screen of heavy planks had been erected before the lower course of its windows and guards with fixed bayonets were posted around its walls at intervals of about twenty feet. An evil odor breathed from it, a smell that impressed itself over the reek from the chimneys and the stink of the trampled mire underfoot—the frowst and stench of human bodies long unwashed, of rotten rags, of sickness. Only a few citizens gathered about to gawk, and these few held their peace.

The guards cried silence. A short, corpulent, black-avised officer bustled out the door and took his station on a horse-block.

"We keep a prison here," he announced in a confident, bullying tone. "None of you has any rights while you're in it, and I'll brook no whining and no fine talk. We'll feed you whatever we have to give you—'tis choicer than what you've been used to, belike—and you'd best be glad of it. Play me any Yankee tricks and you'll rue it in the black hole. Now march in by twos! God save the King!"

The main guard was quartered in the wide vestibule at the base of the spire. The pews and other furnishings had been removed from the body of the church and a flooring of planks supported by wooden posts had been laid across from one gallery to the other, thus providing a second level or precinct for the housing of prisoners. Cleared passages were marked with whitewash on the stone flagging of the lower level, along which the men on watch might move among the hundreds of indistinct figures who sat or lay on the pavement. Every foot of space seemed occupied, yet by thrusting the older prisoners this way and that, the jailors made places for the newcomers.

John perceived, with a decline of the hopeful spirit

which had supported him thus far, that there was little likeness between the rough but careless and indifferent soldiers who had escorted the prisoners on the march and these heavy-handed Provost's men. Spite was writ large on their pitiless faces, and cunning too, and a perverse pride in their work.

He found himself squatted down in the dimness among men with matted hair that hung to their shoulders, beards in all stages of growth, and rags of clothing thick like their skins with grime. The poor wretch next him put out a hand in welcome, made as if to speak, and then bent double in a sharp seizure of coughing.

"Where was you took?" he managed to ask at last. "What's your name?"

"We're of Huntington's reg'ment," the scarecrow went on after John had answered him. "Cap'n Bissell's comp'ny. We was took on Long Island. Jonathan Tyler's my name."

"You've a bad rheum. The surgeon should look to it."

"Let be the surgeon," answered Tyler in his croaking voice. "I'm minded to die on my own terms. If they'd only keep this barn warm, my chest'd be sound in a day or two. See there!" He pointed with a skinny finger to the center of the prison where a fireplace had been built of bricks and iron plates. "They lights it for to cook our rations. Other times we freezes."

These men had been captured on Long Island in August. Only three months in prison had brought them to this pass; had turned solid, upstanding countrymen into dull-eyed vagabonds, wracked with disease and picking at the lice in their rags.

CHAPTER FIVE

ARLY NEXT morning, the men taken at Fort Washington were ordered into line and led to the guard room to be questioned and enrolled. None disobeyed the order, since only those whose names were entered on the prison log would receive a regular ration of food. They had dined on moldy biscuit and water and wished for no closer acquaintance with hunger. Thrice a week, so the older prisoners told them, they would draw their ration—a pound or two of salted pork and sea-bread, with a gill of rice or peas. The guards lit a fire on issue day and stew-kettles were set out; however, it were wiser to save the victuals raw. A man was less tempted then to gorge his entire ration at one meal.

Just ahead of John on the slow moving line, a swaggering fellow from the lower counties of Pennsylvania growled out a ceaseless mutter of complaint. He was a gentleman and an officer, by his own statement; he should have been released on parole, and so he would tell these ministerial jackals. Mere rustic chuffs and mechanics might rot here whilst they waited for an ex-

change but he would not. He would have his rights if he
died for them.

The examination of prisoners was being conducted by
a starch, young officer who sat with two sergeant-
orderlies at a rough wooden table. A fire blazed in an
iron basket behind them. Armed men kept watch in the
guard room and the commandant was also in attendance, standing stiff beside the table with his arms folded
across his chest and a lowering look on his swart face. As
each prisoner came up, he was asked his name, his town,
and the regiment and company in which he had served.
The orderlies wrote the answers down, the one on a
sheet of foolscap, the other in a great book like a merchant's ledger. After the orderlies had done, the officer
took up the questioning. He detained some men longer
than others, as John noticed, and showed them a paper
which several appeared to sign.

When it came the Pennsylvanian's turn to face the
inquisitors, he demanded a parole in a truculent tone
and at length. The officer listened, shrugged, and asked
for proofs of his assertions.

"Proofs, sir! What proofs? I tell you all this on my
honor."

"Honor, sirrah!" broke in the commandant. "There's
impudence for you! Now damme, if you ever led a file.
Not even in the rebel rag and bobtail."

"Do you give me the lie, you tun-bellied lobster?"
The prisoner started forward with fists clenched and
raised. The commandant only lifted his hand. Instantly,
one of the redcoats on guard drove the butt of his
musket into the shouting man's body; his breath went
out of him and he fell, gasping, to the stone floor.

Even before this brutal show, John had determined to hold his tongue. The proofs of his own rank and status were in the pocketbook which some nameless Hessian had purloined, and it was plain that no man's unsupported word would be credited in this place. Moreover, he had another, and a compelling, reason for silence. If he declared himself a surgeon and the British should believe him, they would surely limit his parole and bind him to serve in their own hospitals. The freedom which he craved, and hoped to have so soon as a chance of escape offered, would be sacrificed to no purpose. To be free was all, he felt—free to move at his own will after months of orders and blind obedience, free to consider in quiet the perplexing medley of ideas and experiences which had crowded in on his mind since the day of Concord. Unexpectedly, and with a nagging sense of shame, he was reminded of another who had wished to be free of the war and all that it entailed upon a man's spirit—Shawcross, the shirker and coward. The poor creature's voice rang in John's ears again, pleading to be sent to Fort Lee, calling out for pity from the dust of the Kingsbridge road.

"My name is John Frayne," he said, stepping up to the table, "—of Wendham in Massachusetts. I was 'listed in the 12th Regiment of Continentals—in Wade's Company."

The examining officer yawned and ordered the fire to be stirred.

"What brought you out against your King?" he asked, not troubling himself to look up.

"The King has taken away our rights. He's harried us without cause."

They were stale sentiments enough—the very staple of

patriot oratory—and as John had expected, the officer
paid them no heed. He drew a printed paper from a pile
at his elbow and tossed it over to John. "George the
Third," it was headed, "by the Grace of God, of Great
Britain, France, and Ireland, King, Defender of the
Faith—"

"I offer you a form of submission to the Crown—" the
Englishman's voice was bored and hurried as if he were
reciting a long-conned lesson—"the which, if you sign it
in good faith and take service with His Majesty's forces,
entitles you to full pardon for your past rebellion. It is
my duty to warn you that desertion thereafter will be
punished by death."

"I'm thankful, sir, for your offer and your warning,"
John answered, handing the paper back. "I cannot accept."

"And for what reason, pray?"

"A scruple of conscience."

"Pox me, but these clowns are tender of conscience,"
remarked the commandant, petulantly. "Be wary of this
fellow, captain. He's far too fine of speech for a private
of the line."

"Be wary of him yourself," the officer said. "He's in
your charge, not mine. I've nothing more to say to
him."

When he returned to his place in the prison beside
Tyler and the others, John found them eager to hear
how he had fared. The least matters served to amuse
them, and they discussed John's examination over and
over again before either lapsing into apathy or resuming
the restless pacing with which the more spirited among
them sought to divert themselves.

Left to himself at last, John gave thought to his own

predicament. It was much more difficult than he had supposed. An escape from within would be impossible, for the church-prison was too easily kept under observation by the Provost's men. The planks that screened the windows were stout and firmly fixed, and the one other means of egress was through the guard room.

"Do they ever take us out for exercise?" he asked.

"Now and then," replied Tyler, "when they think on it. They march us round the churchyard. 'Tis a comfortable walk among the tombstones, as good as a sermon. Let pass what's in your mind," he added with a shrewd, sidewise look. "You'll never accomplish it. No more than twenty go forth at a time and the Tory Rangers keep the watch outside. A vengeful, currish crew they are; they'll cut you down for the wink of an eye." He paused, considered, and then went on. "Sometimes we're pressed to bury the dead, a dozen of us or so. The corpses are piled in the yard 'til it grows unsightly —then they're all laid away at once by the Ann Street corner."

"Death's a near neighbor here," muttered a deep-voiced man who sat wrapped in a blanket. "The fever kills us mostly."

"Have you no physicians?"

A cackle of ironic laughter greeted John's question.

"Aye," Tyler answered, "there's a leech who comes. Not so often as the parson from the steeplehouse up the street—but he comes."

"There were two of them at first," said the deep-voiced man. "Antil and Oliver were their names. They were Tories but they did what they could. Now we've a dog named Debute who's worse than naught."

"He was stood in the pillory for a quack," put in another prisoner, "right here in New York, the year the Congress met. And now he's sent to physick us, by God!"

All the men rose to this new topic, each adding his bitter note to the bill of complaint. Louis Debute was a cheat and a murderer; he had struck a man with his cane and killed him, right in that corner there; he sold the medicines the British gave him. By Debute's reckoning, no man was sick until he fell in a stupor, or raved with fever, or suffered a mortified limb. Debute had never been known to examine a prisoner. He visited the prison only when he pleased and hurried through it with a scented kerchief held to his nose, pointing to this one and that one among the sick, and ordering them carried to the houses nearby where the battle-wounded were cared for.

John looked about him while they spoke and wondered how soon the plague would visit the place. Some eight hundred men lay cheek-by-jowl in utter filth and breathing a pernicious air. The prison reeked of excrement and bodies long unwashed. A plague must surely come.

And what if it did, he asked himself angrily, except he should take the infection himself and die of it! The sick were the enemy's concern, not his. Suppose he did declare himself a physician and offer to serve in this foul den. Such a callous fellow as the commandant would never believe him; nor had he any assurance that he would be left here to care for his own people even if he were believed. Conscience had played him false before this; it had driven him forth to Concord, it had kept him with the army, it had cost him Alison Cunningham. He would not have conscience deny him his chance of escape and freedom. Doubtful the chance might be, but he meant to take it.

Just before he fell into the uneasy dreaming which was sleep to a hungry and freezing man, he thought of death once again and as ever with a sad wonder rather than with awe. He remembered how he had mused so on the march to Concord and many times since, putting himself questions which had no answers in this world. Of one thing, however, he had now grown assured—each man died twice, the first time slowly in the defeat of ideals and hopes. The second death was irrelevant.

Next morning, going before the commandant, he offered to serve as a physician in the prison on any terms which the Provost might direct. The commandant cursed him for an impudent liar and ordered him to two days' confinement in the cellar dungeon.

Towards noon on Monday, December 16th (as marked by scratches on the stones, made day by day to keep account of time), some two hundred additional prisoners were crowded into the North Dutch Church. More ragged, meager, and cowed even than those who already tenanted the place, they had been transferred to the city from the *Pacific* prison-ship at the Wallabout Bay.

The weather had worsened and was now wet as well as cold. Rheums and chest complaints multiplied and grew malignant among the miserable creatures who huddled on the stone floor; common chilblains became seriously mortified. Debute, the quack doctor, had ceased to attend in the prison but no one succeeded him. Each morning, the jailors made their own account of the mortally sick and caused them to be borne to the hospital houses outside the walls. Many sick men died before they could be removed and the nights were horrid with a constant stir and groaning.

The Provost's men now began to practice refinements of malice and cruelty. On issue day, when the fire was lit and the shivering prisoners sought to crowd close around it, the guards drove the men back to their places with cudgels and bayonets, crying "Kennel, ye dogs! Kennel!" For several days they withheld the ration of rice. They taunted their charges constantly with news of American reverses in the field—the retreat and pursuit of the army across Jersey, its withdrawal beyond the Delaware, and the capture of General Charles Lee at Basking Ridge. They also drove a brisk trade in offal, which those prisoners who had contrived to keep a little hard money purchased of them and consumed before the starving eyes of the less fortunate. A beef bone with a few shreds of meat clinging to it was sold for fivepence.

During a part of the daylight hours, John diverted himself by peering out through the chinks in the wooden barricade that screened the lower windows. He could see something of the churchyard in this way, and of the street beyond—a few houses, and a small building which was the meeting place of the Moravian sect as he remembered. It was neither a wide prospect nor a happy one, for the latest dead still lay unburied in the yard; yet soldiers and civilians passed within his view at times, walking briskly and with purpose, and keeping him mindful of freedom. He had need of such a reminder. As day succeeded day and no chance offered for escape, he suffered a declension of spirits which alarmed him more than the gradual lessening of his physical strength. He had been taken twice to the yard for exercise, but the Rangers on guard had been vigilant as hounds. When men were drafted to bury the dead or to bear the sick away to the hospitals, the sergeants always passed him by. No single circumstance had favored him, yet he could not lose hope; he would run mad if he did. Only hope and resentment sustained him.

The miseries of the month just past had recalled to his mind a great truth which his first rage over the betrayal of Fort Washington had obscured. The British were still the enemy, and a brutal and unreasonable enemy. It was at least conceivable that the Congress and their General had acted in honest error, whereas British inhumanity had no excuse. In the sad decline of the day of Concord fight, as he was caring for the wounded and gazing on the dead, he had sworn with all the power and passion of his being that the British must pay for the havoc they had wrought. They had taken up the sword and they must perish by it. To these sentiments he now returned. The conduct of this prison in which he lay was of a piece with the oppressions of Parliament and the first, furious resort to force outside Boston. Each action of the British in America expressed the ungenerous, tyrannical character of a nation which was bankrupt in spirit.

On the nineteenth day of December at about the middle of the afternoon, a sergeant and some rankers of the Provost's guard made the rounds of the prison and chose men at random to dig graves. This time the choice fell on John.

"Up with ye!" cried the sergeant, seizing him by the collar. "We've a mort of carrion waiting out beyant."

The chill, fresh air turned John almost faint as he stepped through the door and into the churchyard. A thin fall of snow had just ceased after powdering the earth and the gravestones. The low, sullen sky was brownish-gray and looked laden with storm to the eastward, yet John felt a joy in the open that no springtime day of balmy airs and leafing trees had ever roused in him. Each common thing seemed an intimation of freedom that stirred his blood like a trumpet-call—the crunch of the frozen ground beneath his boots, the reek of chimney-smoke, even the lean dog that coursed outside the fence that bounded the yard.

The illusion of freedom was soon over, for the Provost's men were relieved by a guard of Tory Rangers. Smart and trim in short, red coats and leathern caps tricked out with a cock's feather, the Rangers stood close about the laboring prisoners, and took post at intervals of about four feet.

Facing southward as he plied his spade, John noticed that the palings of the fence along Fair Street were broken down at a point just opposite the mouth of the lane beside the Moravians' meetinghouse. It was little more than fifty paces from where he stood to that break in the fence but it might have been a thousand miles for all the chance he had of winning his way thither. Stealing a look at the Ranger nearest him, John recalled

Tyler's judgment of that corps. Nothing, he was sure, would please this redcoat more than an excuse to use his bayonet on a rebel.

"Dig, ye long-faced rogues!" The officer commanding the Rangers aimed a kick at one of the prisoners as he spoke. "We don't propose to shiver all night at your pleasure."

The fellow had chosen his language well, John thought. In the short time they had been outside the prison, the light had diminished and the sky had become more overcast; the air was heavy with an almost palpable damp. A cutting wind began to howl across the yard. And then, of a sudden, a snow squall swept in from the river to the east. The church, the street nearby, and the guards and the prisoners alike were shrouded and lost in a whirl of white.

Without thought, without plan, still clutching his spade, John darted away in the direction of Fair Street. What might chance after he was past the broken palings, he neither knew nor cared. This was the time, and it might never come again. Lunging heavily against a shadow in the swirling murk, he struck the man down with a blow of the spade. He was through the fence before the hue and cry was raised behind him.

Running hard down the lane alongside the meeting-house, he fancied he heard the noise of pursuit drawing off to the westward; at the John Street corner, as he turned into the teeth of the gale toward Smith Street, he grew certain that the pursuers were on a false scent. This was a fair stroke of fortune. He availed himself of it to slacken his pace. Even in a driving storm, there was danger of arrest if he showed himself in too obvious flight and his shortness of breath and heaviness of limb already made him sensible of the toll that captivity had taken of his strength.

Near the corner of Smith and Crown Streets, he was startled by a discharge of musketry from the direction of the prison and he set off again at a headlong run. Had the prisoners attempted a general escape? Or was the firing intended to alarm any patrols he might encounter? He had seen none as yet, and little street traffic of any kind. A line of commissary wagons rumbled past him up Smith Street but the drivers were too busy with their laboring horses to pay him any heed. In like manner, the few pedestrians, muffled up in great-coats and scarves, who loomed in his path were concerned more with the snow that watered their eyes and stung their faces than with a ragged, running man.

He tarried an instant at Wall Street, considering in a kind of desperation what course he should follow. The City Hall was a few steps to the westward; to the east were the taverns and coffee-houses where the merchants met to drive their bargains. This center of the city's life was no place for a fugitive. And the storm was spending its first rage. The sky was lightening and the snow would soon cease to serve him as a cloak. Men were coming forth from their shops and houses; the first who passed him regarded him with curious stares, hesitated, and then went on. Others would not be so heedless, he thought, and he cursed himself for an indolent fool. He had spent a good month in yearning after freedom like some smock-faced boy yearning after a wench, without once reflecting on what he must do when he had the prize. He was at large, to be sure, but he was weak from starvation and cold; he was wet to the skin; his heart hammered in his body and he felt he could run no more. He knew not a soul to whom he might turn for refuge.

Two sentries were pacing before the City Hall, their heads bowed against the bitter wind; a pair of field pieces flanked the doorway of the building. The British must have established their grand guard in the place and it was a crowning irony that he should have fled there. Even as he thought of this, the door opened and a patrol of redcoats hurried out into the street.

Summoning up all his resolution, for he had been tempted by mere weariness to stand and let them take him, he ran off along Smith Street to Sloat Alley. If the patrol had seen him, the game would soon be over; if not, he could do no more now than race through the snow and hope for an impossible succor.

The alley was a narrow, curving byway, lined on one side with tall and gloomy storehouses and on the other showing the backs of buildings which fronted on a street beyond—houses of some pretension they appeared to be, with small, snow-shrouded gardens and heavily shuttered windows. In the basement of the third house from the Smith Street corner, a door was swinging open and shut as the blasts took it. He had just strength enough to clamber over a low, locked gate, to reach the shelter of the doorway, and to secure the door behind him with a hasp, before his legs failed him. He half-stumbled, half-fell down a flight of steps and sprawled at full length on the earthen floor of a cellar.

While he lay there, breathing in great gasps that

racked his aching chest, he was only a little aware of a commotion in the lane outside—the tread of a numerous body of men and the shouting of commands. By the time he had revived sufficiently to recognize his danger, the noise had grown less. The patrol was pushing its search further on, yet he lay rigid and tried to stifle his sobbing breath even after the sound of the hunt had died away.

The cellar was cold and damp and totally dark. The house above stairs was quiet. It might well be abandoned, he told himself hopefully. Many New York houses had been left so, the while their prudent owners settled themselves at a safe remove from the fighting and waited to see who would win. He rose to his feet at last and began to move cautiously forward, extending his hands before him and feeling about in the dark for guidance. He touched some casks, great ones like tuns, but they sounded empty when he rapped them with his knuckles. He next encountered a pile of wood, cut neatly for fuel, and armed himself from it with a stout cudgel. All around him, he heard rats scurrying.

He had advanced some twenty feet, with still no indication of the character of the house since the rest of the cellar seemed vacant, when he heard footfalls overhead —heavy, confident, a man's tread. Alarmed, he stepped backward but his foot turned under him and he fell. The club in his hand swung wide and hit against one of the casks with a noise like a drumbeat.

He was up again, standing on the defensive with every muscle tensed, when he heard a key turn and the squeak of an ungreased hinge. The door to the cellar had been

opened. It appeared, if he could judge from the sound,
to lie at the head of steps about ten paces to his right.
No light showed but the stair-treads creaked as someone
began to descend.

CHAPTER SIX

A BEAM OF light was flashed out suddenly from a
dark lantern, wavered an instant, and then shone
full on John's face. The householder, if such the in-
truder was, had halted at the foot of the steps. As John's
eyes recovered from their first dazzle, he could see in
the reflection from the whitewashed walls that his ad-
versary was a bulky man and tall.

"Who are you? What are you doing here?" The questioning voice betrayed no alarm; there was a note of
mastery in it.

John tried to speak and could not. The excitement of
the escape had hitherto sustained him but now he felt
drained of all strength and courage. This fellow was
either foe or friend, he told himself desperately; the
chance was even and he must take it.

"Who are you?" the other repeated.

"An American," John answered, letting the cudgel
drop to the floor. "I've escaped from the North Dutch
Church. My name is John Frayne."

"Then you've come to the wrong shop, my man. I'm a
loyal subject of King George, God bless him—I've a pis-

tol in my hand," he warned as John stooped to recover the cudgel, "and I'm not too squeamish to use it. Put your hands above your head. Come forward. Now go up the stairs."

At the head of the steps, the lantern played briefly over a large room that ran the width of the house and was fitted out with easy chairs and small tables on which pamphlets and journals were scattered. A line of tall, closed presses for clothing stood along one wall; opposite them, a flight of stairs rose in a curve to the floor above. As his captor directed the light thither, John supposed that he must continue on upward and did so, coming to a stand in a hallway before a closed door.

"Open it and go in," commanded the voice from behind him.

He stepped into a sitting-room, small but handsomely furnished, and lighted by a number of candles in glass sconce candlesticks. A circular table of mahogany wood first drew his famished eye, for it bore the remains of a dinner on chinaware ornamented with flower-sprigs in color, and a decanter also and glasses. A fire burned low but grateful in a deep fireplace below a chimney-mirror.

At a writing table beside the wall, a man was seated at work over a bundle of papers. He looked around as John entered, showing a lean face, wrinkled and shrewd, with a great jutting nose and cool, dark eyes, ever on the dart like a bird's. In his plain, sad-colored clothes, wearing his own gray-sprinkled hair in a queue, he might have been a tradesman or a merchant's clerk.

"Here's a rat I've caught in the cellar," announced John's captor. He also was a man in middle life, as John could now see—stout of build and hale, his face fleshy and florid, his blue eyes prominent under bushy, white brows. His coat was dark green and heavily laced, his waistcoat was embroidered in green and gold, he had frills to his shirt and ruffles at his wrists, and his bag-wig might have come that very day from the peruke-maker.

"He's a rebel prisoner, as he tells it, escaped from the Provost's hands," the captor continued, quenching the dark lantern and motioning John to stand in the center of the room. "What shall we do with him?"

"He's lean and dirty enough to be telling the truth," answered the man at the writing table, putting down his pen and surveying John from head to foot. "What think you, Oliver?"

"There are tricks in all trades, to be sure."

"Aye, aye. But we'd best hear him speak for himself." The dark-eyed man took a silver snuff-box from his waistcoat pocket and provided himself with a pinch. "Puff off your tale to us, fellow," he ordered.

John wondered how long he could keep his feet, for his head had begun to swim. The sight of the food was more almost than he could bear. He thought of begging for a taste of bread, yet he would not give these two the satisfaction of denying it to him.

"Why should I bide your questions?"

"Because it would be well for you," the dark-eyed man replied mildly, but his look belied his tone. "What is your name?"

"John Frayne."

"So he told me in the cellar," put in the man called Oliver. "He said he was lodged in the church on Fair Street."

"What did you in the rebel army?"

"I was surgeon to the general hospital."

"Where?"

"At Cambridge and in New York. My field duty was with the 12th Massachusetts."

"Where were you taken?"

"At Fort Washington. Look you—" John burst out, "I'm starved and sick. Give me up, if you mean to, but don't torment me with talk."

"Zounds, man," cried Oliver, his face reddening even more, "do you dare dictate to us! Here's my friend William Mooney and me, respectable merchants both, whose trade's been ruined by you murdering Liberty Boys. If I had my way, you'd swing."

"Then have it. Call the patrol and be done with me." John felt a hysteria mounting in him but he was careless now. "Respectable, do you call yourselves? You lie. Many good men are serving the King and think that we do wrong, but you're not of them. We had your like at home—engrossers of land, dealers in black men, forestallers of grain—politic, easy rogues who'll turn a penny no matter how. You'll fawn on the British so long as it pays, even if they torture and kill your countrymen. Here in your own city, under your own eyes, men die daily of hunger and cold in the jails and the prisonships. Were you aught but money-changing scum, you'd cry to heaven against it."

"No more!" shouted Oliver, waving the pistol. "A truce to your treason and lies."

"Hold, Oliver!" the dark-eyed man interrupted. And then to John: "Suppose we were mindful to help you, what would you ask?"

"To go home," John answered dully. He had spent himself in his outburst; the room seemed to spin and sway before his eyes and he was barely conscious of what he was saying. "Only to go home—to think—"

"Why should we trust you? You offer us nothing in proof."

"I cannot. They stole what I had."

"Who commanded the 12th Massachusetts?"

"Colonel Moses Little."

"What townsman was he?"

"Newburyport."

"Who was captain of the second company?"

"Aaron Henshaw, I think—of Dedham."

"Where were Little's when last you saw them?"

"In Jersey, at Fort Lee, with Nixon's Regiment. They'd suffered at Long Island and Harlem; there weren't many of them left. That was more than a month ago—"

The questioner took another pinch of snuff.

"Oliver will lodge you here," he said at last. He waved a hand toward the table. "Eat something."

At night in the prison, John had dreamed of food. Now, with leave to feast on pickled oysters, pigeon pie, and a roast of mutton, he wished for nothing but sleep. His stomach rebelled as he gazed down at the table and he took only a morsel of bread and a glass of Madeira. Between the wine and the warmth of the fire he grew giddy; he would have fallen if Oliver had not caught him. Half-led, half-carried up a flight of stairs and then up another, narrower set of steps to an attic room, he was taken in the dark to a pallet and wrapped in blankets and a quilt. The last thing he remembered was the sound of the attic hatch closing and the rasp of a thrown bolt.

He woke to find Oliver bending over him and shaking him gently. By the light that entered at a dormer window, he judged that it was late afternoon. He had slept near a round of the clock.

"I came up as soon as it was safe," said Oliver. "My workmen and the servants were below 'til now and there's none of them I trust. Here—" and he offered John a bowl of meal pudding and milk, "—breakfast on this. 'Twill sit better in a starved belly than the cates we gave you last night. I must ask your pardon too, for all we said and did to you. 'Twas needful as you'll see, for we play a deep game, do William Mooney and I. You may thank God, by the way, that William was private with me. I thought you were sent by the British to trick us and would have given you up, but William was able to test you. He knows the history of every regiment on the establishment. My name is Oliver Higgins," he went on while John devoured the pudding, "—a merchant tailor of this city. William keeps a furniture shop on Nassau Street. We turned our coats last April by order of the Whig Committee of New York and ranged ourselves with the King's friends. 'Twas believed that we might gather news here in secret if the city were lost to the enemy, and so it's turned out. William has men on watch along every wharf and slip, and the rattles of the British staff have made a club of my shop."

He had much else to tell. The great fire of the past September had destroyed nigh on five hundred build-

ings in the quarter east of Fort George and all along the
west side of Broadway from Beaver Lane to Barclay
Street. To shelter their soldiers and their women, the
British had seized on the houses of every known Whig.
The Tories who had fled during the American occupa-
tion of New York were returning now and clamoring
for redress. General James Robertson was commandant
of the city. He was an old, crippled rake who had made a
mean fortune in years past as a barrack-master, but he'd
put a stop to plundering and was rationing food, fuel
and forage so that all might have a share. Trade was
brisk in stores for the King's ships and the army, and
also in fresh food-stuffs from the Long Island farms. The
North Dutch Church was no worse prison than the
Provost jail, the Bridewell, or the two sugar-houses. All
were abominable but nothing could be done about
them.

Washington's army had indeed retreated beyond the
Delaware, but Higgins scoffed at the notion that this
meant an end of rebellion. "They've bent back the
spring," he said confidently, "but they've not broken it.
The recoil may surprise 'em. Besides, we've forces still
under arms in the Hudson Highlands and in West-
chester. Which minds me, sir, of your own situation.
Take heart. You'll be back with the army within a week.
If our plans go right, we'll be able to pass the whole of
Congress through the enemy's lines by then."

"You've mistook me," John said. "I shan't return to
the army."

He watched his host's expression alter from wonder to
disapproval as he tried to explain his resentment over
the sacrifice of Fort Washington and his wish to return

to Wendham. So be it, he thought. Higgins had been frank and open with him; he could not in conscience deceive the man.

" 'Tis a fine point of morality you've drawn," said Higgins when John had finished. "I'd have expected that your month in prison would have blunted it somewhat. And what will Sir William Howe be doing while you wrestle with your conscience at home? I beg of you," he hurried on, preventing John from speech, "to allow that you might be mistaken. General Washington is a man like ourselves; he cannot see all and know all."

John sat sullen and made no answer.

"If you still believe that our struggle is just," Higgins added, almost casually, "you could be of use to us here. The Tory merchants are swarming back to New York like flies to a molasses barrel. They look to prosper by supplying the King's forces and by selling off the prizes of war which the navy will take. The whole business of the British army will be done in their counting-houses and a man of learning like yourself could easily get work with one of them as a confidential runner. The surest signs of an army's intent are its shipments of supplies— and who'll be better advised of these than the clerk who pens the invoices? General McDougall and young Captain Hamilton shaped out a plan for forwarding such intelligence before the city fell. There'll be hazard in the task, but glory too. Pray think on it."

"My mind's made up," John answered stubbornly. "If you don't choose to help me, I'll risk an escape by myself."

"Have no fear. I'll see you safe out of the city." Higgins's good-humored face had grown stern and con-

temptuous. "If the British catch you, they'll hang you—
and I've no wish for that, whatever your sentiments be.
I saw a young man hanged here last September—a
Ranger from Connecticut named Hale. The British
took him in their lines and hanged him for a spy. Before
he died, he said two splendid things—the one I learned
of by report, the other I heard with my own ears. 'Every
kind of service which is necessary to the public good becomes honorable by being necessary,' he said. And just
before he suffered: 'I only regret that I have but one life
to lose for my country.' "

" 'Twas the speech of an enthusiast," John replied. "I
heard of it, and of him. But no man is called to such an
extreme."

"One evidently was," said Higgins. "I must go now.
Keep as quiet as you can. There's a traffic of redcoats
through my shop and they're not all fools."

Throughout the long day of tedious waiting, John
sought to escape again, this time from himself. Reason
and interest dictated his return to Wendham but a vision disputed them—the vision of a young man standing
before the paraded files, speaking proudly of country
and duty, swinging at the last slowly at the end of a
rope. Dead. Dead before he had lived.

How often must he be thwarted by such vain and de-
lusive fancies, he asked himself passionately? What foolish strain in his blood compelled him to acts which his
reason rejected? He was no firebrand like his brother
Richard, no zealot like Hale. He was a man of science, a
man of peace. When the company formed for the march
at Wendham, he should have turned his back and gone
into his house. And once returned from Concord fight,

he should have stayed snug at home as so many others had done. He had performed his full duty already, and more; he had earned a respite. But the vision of the hanged man persisted, and at last prevailed.

Higgins returned to the attic late that evening with a dinner of bread, cheese, bacon and strong beer.

"The King's friends lack for nothing," he said with a chuckle as John fell to by the light of the dark lantern. "The Commissary serves us well. There's been but little news today. Some say that Newport's been taken. Three ships made port—two of them laden with coals against the freezing weather—"

"What would you have me do?" asked John. "I shall stay in New York as you wish."

"Now God be thanked!" exclaimed Higgins gleefully, "for I've learned just now of the very place for you. Hugh Gaine, the printer, is seeking a shopman. He's a widower like myself, is neighbor Hugh—an Irishman from Belfast who's been long established here. The British have adopted his press as their own; they publish his *New York Gazette* as a Tory journal. Tryon, who was the King's governor of the Province, writes for it; so do Doctor Inglis of Trinity Church, and one Serle who's secretary and factotum to Lord Howe, the Admiral. They needs must keep friend Hugh in charge because he's a printer and a man of business, but they don't quite trust him. Nor would I, in their shoes," went on Higgins, laughing. "All the last fall, whilst his *Gazette* was spouting loyalty here in town, the sly tyke was putting forth another version of the paper in Jersey that was just as hot for liberty, the Congress, and independence. He's a sharp one, to be sure, but we'll outsharp him."

John protested that he knew nothing of the writer's craft or the printer's mystery. Gaine and his friends would detect the imposture at once.

"Nay, not at all," Higgins answered. "You're fashing yourself to no purpose. They have their men to work the press—two journeymen and a boy. 'Tis a poor, harmless, learned drudge that Gaine is seeking; one who can mind the shop, read proofs, and mend his grammar. Moreover, I'll vouch for you and we'll find you a proper disguise."

Higgins mounted to the attic next morning early with a breakfast of cider, bread and ham; descending, he returned with a threadbare coat and breeches of brown fustian, a plain waistcoat, a broad-brimmed hat, worsted stockings, a pair of heavy, country-looking shoes, and a parcel wrapped in canvas.

"I bring you your new identity," he announced. "Behold the dress and all the worldly goods of Absalom Prentiss, as we've decided to name you—a most unfortunate pedagogue from Norwich in Connecticut whom jealousy and evil tongues caused to be discharged from a school on Long Island. I've given Gaine a pretty character of you, though I fear I hinted that drink was your undoing. No matter. He made no bones of it, nor will anyone else. Men of learning are scarce in New York these days, be they drunk or sober."

John put on the clothes and examined the parcel. It contained some stale bread and cheese, several pens, a pitchpipe, grammars of both Latin and English very dirty and dog-eared, and a psalm-book with the musical notation.

"Inglis and Tryon are famous gossips," said Higgins jubilantly. "You'll overhear more in a day at Gaine's shop than you'd learn in a month as a merchant's clerk. You might even discover how Tryon floods New England with counterfeits of our paper money. It's ruin and bankruptcy unless we can stop him. However, all in good time. Bring me no news 'til I manage a meeting between us. I'll order some trifles from Gaine and you will carry them here. 'Twill be a sufficient excuse. And now let's be off to friend Hugh's."

The ironies of war were many and strange, thought John as he followed Higgins down from the attic. Not the least of them was this late conjunction of his brother Richard's fate with his own. Grub Street had claimed them both. Poor, confident, witty Richard, so firm in his Tory opinions—how he would have relished John's present prospect of plotting and intrigue! Yet he drudged in London for the scant bread of exile while the task had fallen to one who relished it not at all. The situation was farcical like much of life, and tragic too, as life observed in totality was tragic. The ends that he and Richard sought were exactly opposed, yet they had come to the same, mean condition; the loyal supporter of the ordered, reasonable world of their youth, and the troubled skeptic who had thought that the cause of America was the cause of mankind, were alike disappointed. They were become pieces of little worth in a game that others played. And which was the greater fool?

The sun was flooding in through the front windows of Higgins's shop as they passed through it to the street.

The British officers had made it a club, so Higgins had said, and the elegant room was well suited to the purpose. Framed mezzotints of military figures hung on the walls, books and journals lay scattered over the tables, and racks of clay pipes were handily disposed. Through a door that opened into a rear room, John could see a number of tailors squatted down by their low benches and hard at work even at that early hour.

"We don't lack for custom," said Higgins in a low voice. "The redcoats give us a deal of it. They crowd this room from noon 'til dinner, and many a curious bit of news I gather from their babble. They're poor pay, however, for they settle accounts in London style— which is to say at a long reckoning. 'Twas otherwise before the war. The gentlemen of New York never stinted themselves either, but their credit was as good as the Bank of England's. We made clothes to measure of our country patrons and sent them by carrier as far as Amboy in Jersey. Superfine cloth too, and in all the modish colors! Solid bullion lace! Magnificent!"

Hanover Square, on which the shop fronted, belied its name for it was triangular in shape—a genteel, tree-shaded enclave off Queen Street, lined with hip-roofed, brick houses of three or four stories. Alongside Higgins's white door with its name-plate of polished brass were two windows; in the one was displayed a fine velvet suit, in the other a bolt of scarlet cloth was draped artfully about a pedestal. Each merchant who kept in Hanover Square announced his trade by a sign that hung just above eye-level on his house—a gilded hammer, a mortar and pestle, a scythe, a ship, and at about four doors' remove from the tailor's shop an open book surmounted by a crown. Many people were abroad in Queen Street and in the lanes that led down to the waterside. At the head of a slip which lay opposite Higgins's house, folk were cheapening goods at a row of stalls beneath a low, wooden shed.

"The Tories are brisk these days, as I told you," said Higgins, surveying the scene. "They were solid men of business once and they hope to be so again. Fifteen new firms of vendue-masters have opened shop over there by the wharves, and a good two dozen chandlers. 'Where the carcase is, there shall the eagles gather,' as the Scriptures say—and truly."

They walked the short distance to the house distinguished by the sign of the open book; it was the sign of the Bible and Crown, as John observed at a closer view. The house was wider than its neighbors and its doors opened directly on the street without the customary three or four steps. Low, wide windows on either side of the door displayed a bewildering array of objects for sale. There were books in bright, new, calf bindings, books in blue paper wrappers, books held open with a ribbon to show a print or a title-page. Toy books for children, chapbooks on coarse paper, playing-cards, shaving soap, balls of shoe-blacking, gloves, spectacles, and a jumble of jars and vials containing cosmetics and patent medicines. A placard in one window announced that Mr. Gaine had also for sale a parcel of choice hog's fat in small kegs; in the other window, the public were similarly reminded that Mr. Gaine paid up to fourpence a pound for good linen rags.

"Nothing is beneath Hugh's notice," remarked Higgins, answering John's unasked question. "He's a printer by trade but he's a chapman at heart. He's sold everything at one time or another—from knives and forks and silk stockings to a face lotion that cures the vapors. He's sole agent for the great Doctor Keyser's pills that banish all human sicknesses from belly gripes to the French Pox. His rivals cry shame and they blush for the book trade, but Hugh cares nothing for their opinion."

"He's a rascally quack!" exclaimed John, hastily scanning the goods in the windows. "The trash I see here could poison half the town."

"Gently, sir, gently," Higgins replied. "You must put off the physician if you mean to work for Hugh Gaine. Pray recall that you're Absalom Prentiss now, a poor, drunken ass of a schoolmaster. Keep a rein on your tongue or you'll have us all in the suds."

The shop was a deep, spacious room, furnished with shelves along the walls and deal tables on which books and other merchandise in which the printer dealt were set out in neat order. At the back, near a closed double door, was a little, railed-off space with a desk and a chair on which a stocky, pursy-faced man in a scratch-wig was seated. He rose as his visitors entered, pushed his spectacles up on his forehead, closed the ledger over which he'd been poring, and then hastened forward. He wore a plain serge coat and small-clothes, rather slovenly in look as John thought, a linen neckcloth, and shoes with polished steel buckles.

"This is most kind of you, neighbor Higgins," he said, seizing Oliver's hand and wringing it warmly. "I'm half distracted with business, and never a soul to help me. Is this the young man we spoke of?"

"Prentiss will serve you well," said Higgins after he had made John known to his new master. "He's a quick lad, and honest. Best of all, he's a loyal subject—'twas his loyalty, indeed, that cost him a fine place in Connecticut. As for his late difficulty on Long Island—" Higgins paused, shrugged and looked grave.

"We'll say no more of it," Gaine broke in. "We're all of us human, and some of us more than others. The man who's never tried is never proved. Mind you—" he continued, looking hard at John, "I'll stand for no tippling in my house. What's bygone is bygone, to be sure, but we part at once if you take to the bottle again. This dram-drinking is a fearsome thing. I'd an uncle by marriage once—but let that be. Sit ye down at my desk yonder and show me a sample of your hand of write. Make a fair copy of the topmost draught on that pile. 'Tis only a note to my papermaker."

He was praising John's work a few moments later when a tall, slightly stooped man entered through the door at the rear of the shop. The newcomer was dressed in a rich suit of black; he had a spare, dark, stern face under his white wig, and deepset, weary eyes.

"I beg the favor of presenting Oliver Higgins to you, Mr. Serle," said Gaine with deep deference. "He is a good friend to government, and a—"

"I know Mr. Higgins by repute," Serle answered in a low, pleasant voice. "My compliments to you, sir."

"And this is the young man he recommends to be my shopman."

Serle looked sharply at John as Gaine pushed him forward.

"I'm told you're a schoolmaster," he said. "Have you

letters from your late employers, or from your clergy-man?"

"I had them once, your honor," replied John in a tone of complaint. "They were stolen from me on Long Island as I journeyed hither. 'Twas some of His Majesty's German soldiers that took them from me—and a pocketbook too that they were in, along of eighteen shillings paper, and a tobacco box, and two shirts almost new."

"Those plundering dogs rob friend and foe alike," said Serle to Gaine in anger. "Sir William is at his wit's end to curb them. The Hessians have cost us more friends in the Jerseys than all the blether of Congress. I'm sorry for your loss, my good fellow," he continued, turning to John. "All men suffer in a civil conflict like this one. As Horace says:

> *'Quis non Latino sanguine pinguior*
> *Campus sepulcris impia proelia—'"*

He waited, expectant. John promptly capped the verses:

> *" 'Testatur auditumque Medis*
> *Hesperiae sonitum ruinae?' "*

"Excellent!" Serle exclaimed. "And how close the old Roman hath hit it! The French look on and gloat while we tear ourselves to bits. And all for no good reason. Why are the rebels in arms, think you?"

" 'Tis for their liberties, as they say," answered John cautiously, "but I doubt it."

"And well you might," Serle continued on a note of enthusiasm. "These colonies were ever allowed more liberty than the Constitution of Britain permits by its nature. America has never paid a thirtieth part of the taxes that are paid by our people at home. All the present troubles stem from that generous laxity. No region on this earth—Great Britain not excepted—can boast of equal endowments and privileges. I challenge any man to prove me the contrary. And as for representation in Parliament—! I ask you, sir, as a man of sense, would it not be foolish to entrust the very being of the Empire to the whims and decisions of men from subordinate places—men of necessity lacking in information and breadth of mind? The House of Commons would be no better than the Polish Diet, where any man's voice can frustrate the most delicate policies."

" 'Tis surely as you say," agreed John. "Our politicians at home were a sorry lot."

"We shall get on well together," said Serle. "Your principles are admirable. You may hire this man," he told Gaine. "Doctor Inglis and Governor Tryon will take my word for him. And now—I am your servant, gentlemen—" Donning a cloak which he had brought with him on his arm, he went out into the street.

"Well, well, oh very well!" exclaimed Gaine. "Master Serle is a difficult man to suit and I thought I'd be waiting long for a helper. I'll pay you four shillings a week, Prentiss, and I'll board you. You can sleep in the attic; it's warmer than the shop. Do you like the terms?"

John nodded agreement.

"Then we're master and man, and I'm glad on it. You'll have the attic all to yourself, for the prentice laddie lives with his mother and the journeymen are unthrifty rogues who insist on boarding elsewhere. By day, you must mind the shop and wait on custom—but give

no credit without you ask me first! We've sad dogs
about, and some of them wear red coats. Fare you well,
neighbor Higgins," he called to Oliver who was quietly
taking leave. "I owe you a kindness for this. Pray call on
me! These books on the front tables," he continued, resuming his instructions to John and hustling him forward, "are the staples of the trade. The price is writ in
every volume and no one's to have a discount. Here's
Pilgrim's Progress in calf neat, and over there a cheaper
edition. Here's *The Whole Duty of Man*—Mr. Pope's
poems—Fordyce's Sermons—aye, and Shakespeare too.
We've had much call for playbooks since the Army's
come to town. Over on these shelves are the last imports
from London—mere rubbish, the most of them, but they
sell. Doctor Goldsmith's a noble exception, to be sure,
and Samuel Johnson's another. Great intellects, lad,
great wits are they both, and salable to boot. Here's Mr.
Sterne complete. He sells too, let be his morals. While I
think on it," he interrupted himself, looking critically
at John, "you must buy a wig like mine and wear it. We
have a genteel custom here. Besides, it's a rebel affectation to wear one's own hair. We loyal folk must put it
down, if only to help the peruke-makers."

John promised to do so, and added that he feared he
had much to learn of the book trade.

"Much to learn!" Gaine rolled up his eyes and spread
his hands. "Everything, everything! The books are only
the beginning. There's the face-paints and the medicines to know of, the cutlery and the toys, the gloves and
stockings in those boxes yonder, the pocketbooks and
tea canisters and blacking-balls—aye, and the market
price of goods that folk bring in to barter. But I'll be

patient with ye. 'Tis Serle and Inglis and Governor
Tryon who'll try your soul. Be wary of them, lad. Do
just as they bid you. I needs must jump when they
whistle myself. Say naught but praise of what they write
in the *Gazette* and change not a jot of it, for they're all
three as arrant authors as ever I've met. Have you ever
read proofs for the press? Ah well, there's no great knack
to it. Just see that the print agrees with the manuscript,
word for word and point for point. My printing-office is
here at the back." He led John down to the double door
and threw it open. "Two presses—English Common."
He spoke almost with affection as he pointed in at them.
"As fine as any in the colonies."

The printing room was about two-thirds the size of
the front shop but it looked smaller by reason of the
clutter within it. A roaring fire blazed in a fireplace at
the left; the light that entered through four grimy windows was supplemented by a number of candles in tin
sconces. Tall wooden cases for storage of type were
ranked along the walls. Gaine's journeymen and the ap-
prentice were all at work around one press, spreading
the ink, pressing the platen down on the chase, and
drawing off the freshly printed sheets which they hung
up to dry on overhead racks. Piles of blank paper, fresh
from the wetting trough, were ready to their hands. The
air was heavy with a curious scent, part linseed oil, part
the resin of pine.

"Printer's ink," Gaine said, drawing in a long breath
through his nose. "There's no smell in the world to
match it."

II

NEW YORK: AT THE BIBLE AND CROWN

January, 1777

CHAPTER SEVEN

THE SUN shone weakly in a pale sky on the morning of December 30th, 1776. Queen Street was treacherous underfoot with trampled and frozen snow. The horses that drew the drays and army wagons along the rutted roadway slipped and stumbled to a music of cracking whips and teamsters' blasphemies.

John had taken proofs of the *Gazette* to Ambrose Serle's lodging in Smith Street, and now, as he was trudging back to Gaine's shop, he stared all about him like any curious yokel. During his previous stay in New York, the city had been under siege—a drab, sick, miserable place; today, a restless and buoyant spirit possessed it. The Fly Market stalls were scant of goods, yet people gathered there if only to gossip, or to trade in whispers at prices forbidden by General Robertson's proclamation of fair dealing. There was no lack of money. The Tory merchants, as Higgins had foretold, were mending their fortunes by any means and all. The silversmiths were flourishing, and the wine-merchants; the Coffee House and the Exchange were thronged with buyers and sellers. Christmas had been kept as a high festival

105

with feasting and general mirth. Each day, during guard mount outside the City Hall, a band of music played and a concourse of soldiers and civilians assembled with their ladies to watch the ceremony. After the curfew gun was fired at eight o'clock, the city was officially at rest but the publicans knew better.

The legend "G.R." was inscribed in red paint on many of the doors that John passed between Maiden Lane and Wall Street. The finer of these houses had been confiscated for use as officers' quarters (Colonel Clark of the 7th Regiment had one all to himself); the lesser of them were occupied by married sergeants and the families of common soldiers. Troops of children ran in and out in noisy, happy play and slattern women looked down from the windows to bawl advice and warnings.

Prolonging his walk, for he was not needed immediately at Gaine's, John continued on down Dock Street past the hardware and salters' shops around the head of Coentie's Slip, past the Queen's Head tavern at Broad Street and the Exchange, almost to Whitehall. Thereabouts, and westward across the tip of Manhattan, all lay in ruin save for the partially dismantled fort by the Bowling Green and a few fine houses nearby it where General Robertson and his staff were quartered. The ravage of the past September's conflagration was still unrepaired, although rude shelters of timber and sailcloth were beginning to rise here and there amid the tumbled walls. To the eastward, however, the wharves and piers were teeming with life and business. Shipmasters in shore-going broadcloth stalked along in full consequence; coopers and riggers were loud and profane at

their work; harried clerks scrambled about with mani-
fests clutched in their hands. Carters urged their nags
down the quays between piles of green truck brought
over on market-boats from Long Island, pipes of wine,
hogsheads of sugar, molasses and rum, casks of sea-bread,
and crates of muskets and small-arms. A line of black
men chanted in rhythm as they lifted corded bales from
the hatches of a tall Indiaman and passed the cargo
down to the pier. A smart barge, rowing in from one of
the men-of-war, scraped its varnish against a dingy sloop
and the officer lounging in the stern-sheets howled with
rage. Amid the scurrying of sailors and civilians, idle
soldiers of the garrison sauntered and gawked—fusiliers
in scarlet, gunners in dark blue, Hessian chasseurs in
green and silver lace, kilted Scotsmen of the 42nd Regiment.

John turned and walked back to Hanover Square. As
he passed Broad Street, curving out of Dock Street to his
left, he watched a lady alight from her carriage before
one of the handsome residences there, her servants carrying her across the mire to the doorstep. A little further on, by Old Slip, a sleek crowd of speculators waited
before a shop where a vendue was advertised.

The sense of physical vigor and well-being which he
had experienced for most of the fortnight past was something more, he thought, than a response to freedom
after captivity; the city had communicated to him a little of its own renewed life. He felt himself a favored
spectator at a grand, tragic drama—so much so that he
was forgetful at times of the part he had to perform in
it. The British officers who congregated at Gaine's shop
were those who set up for wits; they were at once

cleverer and less discreet than the fashionables who had
their club at Higgins's establishment. Talk was their life
and intrigue their element. They ranged in character
from stern, military zealots like Major Robert Donkin
to macaroni cornets and ensigns but lately free of the
schoolroom; they were alike only in the license with
which they criticized everything—poetry, Parliament, the
War Office, and their immediate superiors. Some few of
their number, inspired by one Captain Blythe of the
17th Regiment who was a secretary-aide at Sir William
Howe's headquarters, were preparing a season of plays
to be performed at the theater in John Street; their talk
was all of scenery, costumes, and how Macklin or Gar-
rick walked a part. Others, by their own showing, devoted their leisure to cards and women and exercised
their intellects with the making of epigrams, love songs
and riddles.

Little of any importance had appeared so far in the
gossip at Gaine's. On the two occasions when Higgins
had arranged for him to call and report, John had been
loath to offer the meager intelligence which he had
overheard, but the tailor had listened carefully and
noted the least informations down. Such news was nothing in itself, he observed, but it might well have value
in conjunction with news from other sources. He
showed a greater interest in what John had to say of the
temper and spirit of the junior officers, for it confirmed
what he had himself noticed. Most of them had no stomach for the war. It promised them neither glory nor pelf
and they were concerned to have it over on any reasonable terms. They still believed that the Americans were
a rabble of country fellows unworthy of the name of sol-

dier but they no longer took pleasure in the conquest of so mean a foe. Whatever feelings of patriotic anger they might once have entertained against Americans as rebellious subjects had declined into peevishness against General Washington and the Congress for prolonging a hopeless struggle.

Higgins begged John to persevere, especially in his association with Serle and Doctor Inglis although John had culled nothing from their talk that could not be read in the *Gazette*. The rebellion was an unqualified evil, proclaimed that sapient newspaper; all good men must unite to crush it. And now was the time. The plight of the American army was desperate. Not even the offer of huge bounties could hold the rebel soldiers to their duty; Washington's broken regiments had fled beyond the Delaware only to melt away; the capture of General Charles Lee at Basking Ridge had removed the one officer of distinction from the rebel council of war. The Royal arms were triumphant everywhere in Jersey and the grateful people of that Province were accepting the King's pardon by thousands.

John wondered if Inglis and Serle were themselves deceived by the lies they printed. He doubted it. Serle knew that the Hessian looting and outrage in Jersey had disaffected even the Tories there. Only two days before, Gaine had come to John with a long face and whispered how an entire Hessian brigade had been surprised by Washington at Trenton, defeated, and made prisoners. Rall, their colonel, had been slain in the attack. Serle must surely have known of this—indeed, he had been Gaine's informant—yet the new number of the *Gazette* glossed over the action as a mere skirmish of outposts and devoted the greater part of its columns to what it called a true relation of the state of Pennsylvania. Three-fourths of the people of that Province, it announced, were opposed to the independence of America and would gladly welcome the fall of the criminal faction which had forced that measure on the country. For this opinion, there was no more evidence than the word of a Mr. William Allen, a Tory, who had said as much to Serle in John's hearing.

Despite the tailor's assurances of the value of his service, John was in no wise convinced of it. Moreover, Hugh Gaine exacted from him the last pennyworth of his fee. When John was not straining his eyes over the proofs of the newspaper, or making fair copies of political essays by Inglis and Serle and Governor Tryon, his master set him to taking stock in the shop, to writing out bills and inventories, or to carrying great bundles of chapbooks and pamphlets to the peddlers who hawked them through the Hudson River towns and on Long Island. There was still a brisk trade in such minor literature and Gaine proposed to miss none of it. To cap all, Gaine set a frugal table; the food was poor and far from plentiful.

Hanover Square was lively with shoppers when John arrived there. An elegant carriage was drawn up before the dry-goods warehouse next door to the Bible and Crown and three Dragoon officers waited beside it like dapper attendant spirits. Loungers were pausing as usual to look at the goods in Gaine's windows but only one customer was within—a slim, tall man in uniform who was standing by the fireplace conning a book as John entered and who raised his eyes to stare an instant before he returned to his reading. It was the presiding genius of the theater, Captain Arthur Blythe, but as he said nothing John contented himself with only a slight bow of recognition. Handsome in a black-browed, lowering way, the Captain carried his height with a lounging elegance and was altogether a man to be remarked in any company. A petulant, scornful twist of the mouth was customary with him, however, and gave his face a disagreeable cast.

Gaine had started up from his desk at John's appearance and came bustling forward.

"I've had news of a bargain in muslins at Hunter's Quay," he exclaimed. "You must mind the shop, lad, whilst I run there to secure it. A sorry morning it's been! We've had ladies here and they've tumbled over the whole of the face-paints and perfumes with never a purchase—not so much as a bottle of Hungary water! They've gone off now to make havoc next door in Remsen's shop, God help him! For there isn't a penny to be made of them. Not a penny!"

It was a strange medley of boxes, vials and bottles that John set about restoring to order after the ladies' depredations—rose-water, lip salve, patches, powder puffs, essence of bergamot, Jesuit's drops, and Greenough's tincture for preserving the teeth and gums. Also Lady Molyneux's Italian Paste for enamelling the neck and hands, Dr. Constable's ointment for pimples, and the celebrated Bloom of Circassia "imparting a rosy tint to the cheeks"—or so the label promised—"which will neither rub off, nor be washed away by perspiration."

"Will you forgive me," said a mocking voice in his ear, startling him out of his contemptuous absorption in his work, "if I intrude some business on your studies?"

John looked around quickly. Captain Blythe was at his elbow.

"This playbook," the officer continued, holding out a pamphlet. "I've a fancy for it. Pray, what's the price?"

"Eight shillings, Captain."

"Indeed? Yet the wrapper says only two shillings and sixpence, and in fair print too. The balance must be your master's toll on the public."

"These playbooks are shipped from London, sir," John answered. "The price on the wrapper is the London price. We must amend it here."

"You're an economist too, as I perceive." A warm and unexpectedly pleasant smile lit up the Captain's dark face. "Come sir," he went on, "don't frown on me. Your master's a robber and we both know it, yet you do well to take his part and it need break no bones between us. Place the book to my account. Have you read it, perchance? 'Tis called *The Rivals;* I saw it acted in London last year. The author's a son of old Sheridan, the player —which goes far to prove that wit knows not its father. The genteel characters are naught, but he's filled his tale with humors out of the old comedies and graced it with speeches that make me envy him."

"I should be pleased with it then," John answered eagerly, forgetting his role of country schoolmaster. "I've read some plays of Farquhar and Vanbrugh that I liked well—and Shakespeare's comedies too, although I've never seen them played."

"Be patient a little. We'll enact a whole repertory at John Street theater, if this war lasts long enough. 'Twill not be all comedy, to be sure—and there'll be none of those sentimental follies of Cibber's fashioning or Kelly's that the women run mad after. Nay, sir, we'll have gorgeous tragedy in the chiefest place."

"We studied Seneca at the College," said John, "—'twas his *Thyestes*. And I've read over dramas by Jean Racine which my father had among his books."

"Look you, sir," interrupted the Captain, who had drawn out his watch and marked the time. "I'd as soon talk all day of such matters, but I'm late for duty and I must be off. Take dinner with me tonight and we'll parley at leisure. I dine at five, at Lenox's tavern in Wall Street. Ask for me there."

Blythe had no sooner gone than Ambrose Serle appeared at the door, accompanied by a man much of his own stripe—a thoughtful looking personage, plainly but richly dressed and haughty of manner. They went upstairs at once to Gaine's own sitting-room where John was summoned presently to attend them, one of the pressmen taking his place in the shop.

"Mr. Joseph Galloway of Philadelphia has honored me with some of his thoughts for use in the *Gazette*," said Serle. "Be so good as to minute them down."

John regarded the stranger with a new interest. Once a Whig and a valued member of the first Congress, Galloway had become a leader of the Tory faction. Some of his apologists said that it was over the question of American independence which he could not accept; others, that he was jealous of the dominance in Congress of men whom he considered inferior to himself.

"Mr. Galloway informs me," began Serle after John had set himself to write, "that the detestable rebellion is everywhere broken. The colonies may make further efforts at resistance but these will be feeble and ineffectual. Since the colonies have no manufacturies, they will soon be in distress for want of clothing, dry goods, salt, and all other importable goods. Therefore, if the fleet be steadfast in the blockade of the American ports, the rebellion will collapse no later than next summer for lack of popular support. At that time, if His Majesty's government will provide in writing the draft of a fair and just constitution for the whole of the British empire, all problems will be solved and the rebels will return to their allegiance. Have I stated your views correctly, sir?"

"You must add," replied Galloway in a pompous, measured tone, "that the Assemblies of all the colonies must be convened to examine the constitution as it is written. The Assemblies will set forth any alterations which they feel are necessary, and Parliament will be guided in its final draft of the paper by what the Assemblies will suggest. This is a most important point, my dear Serle."

After Galloway had read what John had written and had approved of it, they returned all three to the shop and the Tory leader took his leave. Serle was most complimentary in his farewells, assuring Galloway of his own gratitude as well as Lord Howe's for so wise and pregnant a statement of policy. But the door had hardly closed before he turned to John a face that was livid with anger and disappointment.

"Damn and blast the fellow!" he cried. "I ask him what measures the Loyalists will take in their own defense, and he gives me a parcel of false guesses and a beggarly lecture on constitutions. Not one word of loyal men in arms for their King, nor of loyal juntoes springing up to challenge the rebel Congress! Not one word of a counter-rebellion! Yet I'm ordered to cherish such cowards; I'm told they're His Majesty's friends. Such talking, law-minded, do-nothing friends are worse than a legion of enemies. You're a plain American, my lad. What think you of this Galloway and his like?" John answered that he knew nothing of such great men and had no skill in judging them. "We must alter our policy," Serle ran on, little heeding what John had to say. "The Loyalists have neither power nor influence. I see that now. Each stands alone and speaks only for himself or for a handful of his friends. I'm persuaded that the great mass of Americans care nothing for either Whig or Tory. They'll follow whoever wins this war, whoever is strong. If Sir William would only throw off his cursed dalliance and crush the rebel army, the whole cabal of Congress and Assemblies and independence would fall to ruin."

He went back into the press-room, slamming the door behind him.

Here was grist for Higgins's mill, John told himself as he resumed his interrupted task. A full measure of it, yea, and running over! If the Tories refused to help themselves, there might still be hope for the American cause. The British must soon tire of a struggle so far from home in which they bore the whole of the burden. And should Washington and his generals be able to prolong the war and evade a decisive battle, the victory might be theirs by default. Was that indeed their strategy? And could the sacrifice at Fort Washington have been a part of the plan, however mistaken and forlorn in its effect? The thought troubled him.

When Gaine returned, he grumbled a little at the time John had taken over the lotions and perfumes but he accepted John's explanation and was vastly pleased to hear of the engagement to dine with Captain Blythe.

"A good stroke, lad," he exclaimed, rubbing his hands. "A friend at headquarters is a friend indeed. You'll fare well with the Captain, and better than you would at home. We're having a cold dinner of yesterday's pork."

It was but a short walk from the shop to Lenox's tavern. The sign-board before the place, creaking in the wind from the river, bore the painted likeness of an Indian chieftain; it was said to represent Brant, the Mohawk. Within, the long room was crowded; the table in the center at which the ordinary was served had not a single place vacant. The host, however, on hearing whom John was seeking, grew suddenly affable and led him to one of the pew-like enclosures or cubicles in the rear by the great fireplace. After setting out a pair of candles on the table and a decanter of Madeira, he informed John that Captain Blythe was never on time for an appointment.

As he sipped at a glass of the full-bodied wine, half-listening to the boisterous talk of the redcoat diners and their friends, John did not grudge the wait. He was enjoying a sense of physical ease and content to which he had long been a stranger. Captain Blythe might already suspect him to be other than he seemed, yet he was so starved for the company of a man of his own degree and tastes that he readily accepted the risks of a closer acquaintance. And there need be no risk at all if he remained discreet and close-mouthed. Serle and Gaine had vouched for him, and Blythe, unless he proved to be a very master of subtlety, seemed too light of character to pursue any suspicions which he might have. The Captain's frank manner, sharp tongue, and air of the great world were not commonly the marks of a spy or a man-catcher.

Blythe strode into the tavern at about a quarter before six.

"Madeira?" he asked, cocking an eye at the decanter. "Excellent. I'll join you in it. Lenox, my man, serve up at once! The commander-in-chief stayed late today," he continued to John, "and was uncommon tedious to boot. Bad luck at the cards, I fancy—he's a monstrous sullen loser—or a tiff last night with his Sultana. But he shan't spoil my appetite, nor shall I spoil yours with any more talk of him."

They dined off roast beef which was very well dressed and served, and no less good for being contraband; a lobster also, and an apple tart. The principal delicacy of the meal, however, so far as John was concerned, was Blythe's conversation. The Captain ranged happily from gossip of the theaters to the small talk of the London clubs, from the latest speculations of the philosophers to the last tête-à-tête in the *Town and Country* magazine. More to the purpose, John learned of him how General Robertson, the commandant of New York, was a fool for young women despite his seventy years; how a host of the younger officers were well on the road to ruin because of their gaming for high stakes; how the army commissaries dealt hand-in-glove with the contractors; and how even Sir William Howe was a sleeping partner in a firm of purveyors.

" 'Tis the way of the world," said Blythe with a laugh on noticing John's expression of distaste. "Sir William has his fortune to make here, just like the rest of them. God knows he's in no way to win glory, so he must even get what he can."

The Captain had been attentive to the wine all during dinner and had grown quite tipsy, leaning a little forward and his eyes staring although the play of his tongue was nothing affected.

"You're a man of extraordinary sensibility," he assured John. "I made up my mind to that when I saw you first in the shop. I'm seldom deceived in such matters. 'Tis one of my few talents. 'Look you, Blythe,' I said to myself, 'you must make a friend of this provincial, for he has sensibility.' A man of feeling should be cherished, d' you see, wherever you find him. He's a precious rarity, even in London, and especially so in this wretched village—this paradise of forestallers, cheats and soldiers." Blythe nodded solemnly, refilled his glass, and continued. "And yet it's a troublesome quality, is sensibility, as you must have learned to your cost. It limits action. It makes you a looker-on at life, and over disdainful of the clods you must live amongst. Haven't you found it so? You can change neither them nor yourself. Now in the theater," he ran on, "a sensible man breathes easier. He can be at home among illusions as he never can be amid the vulgar, petty rogueries of society. The heroes of the playbooks have each a fault, but 'tis a grand, tragic fault such as becomes a man. The women of the drama are true as steel or else false wantons, but surely and greatly so. You've no need to study them or spy them out. The poets have done it for you. Why do I speak of illusions?" he demanded, raising his voice and striking the table hard with the flat of his hand. "The stage is no more an illusion than life at court, and much to be preferred in point of manners. You should give yourself to literature, my friend," he resumed in a quieter tone. "As I should, if I had the courage to sell my commission and disgrace my blood. Better to starve in a Grub Street attic than to fatten in service to Sir William Howe."

He fell silent then, looking down on the table and chewing his lip. Presently they rose to go. As the Captain walked stiff-legged and uncertain, John felt it prudent to accompany him to his quarters in Isaac Roosevelt's house.

Blythe said nothing on the walk up Queen Street, but when they reached the house and John had spoken a few words of gratitude for the dinner and for the Captain's company, he threw off his silent humor.

"We shall dine together again," he said, clutching at John's arm to steady himself. "I mean to be your friend, just as I've told you. And in earnest of that, my dear sir, let me beg of you to study your role of shopman a trifle better or someone who's not your friend will find you out. You're no more a merchant's clerk than I am, nor Prentiss the schoolmaster either. Tell me nothing," he hurried on before John could speak. " 'Tis none of my affair why you're *incognito*. Fate deals us shabby hands at times and we play them as best we can."

CHAPTER EIGHT

HUGH GAINE descended the stairs into his shop early next morning with the look of a man in a temper, and John who was sweeping the floor had not long to wait for a taste of it.

"Draw the covers off the tables and set out the goods," the master ordered gruffly. "Mind you don't idle whilst I'm away. I've done a thing I've sworn never to do—I gave a man my note-of-hand yesterday, and now I must off to Hunter's Quay with the money to buy it back. I've lain awake half the night thinking of it."

He was home again within the hour and in vastly better spirits. But at about the middle of a lecture which he was addressing to John on the evils of buying on credit, even to secure an undoubted bargain in muslins, he was interrupted by the arrival of Ambrose Serle and a lanky, ruddy-faced naval officer.

"Permit me to make Lieutenant Hammond known to you, sir," said Serle to Gaine. "He's an aide to my Lord Admiral, and come but lately from London. I've brought him to see how we manage the press in America."

120

The visitors accepted Gaine's invitation to breakfast. The sailor ate with good appetite but Serle did little more than stir his porridge with a spoon and refused the smoked herrings, contenting himself with a tankard of mulled ale and sitting silent while Gaine held forth on the state of trade and the morning's news among the merchants.

"What's amiss with ye, man?" he demanded of John at last. "Mr. Serle has a chancy stomach, as well I know, but you're used to bolt your victuals faster than this. Ah, now I have it! You've maybe grown over fine for our food after last night's feasting. The lad dined at Lenox's," he explained to Serle. "He was bid there by Captain Blythe who is one of Sir William's writers."

"I could wish him in better company," Serle said.

"Eh, now!" ejaculated Gaine at a nonplus. "Sure, where was the harm in it?"

"There's always harm in a fool's company."

"Is it Arthur Blythe you speak of?" The naval officer looked up from his plate. "You're hard on him, Serle."

"Headquarters is filled with just such fops who've wit and to spare for all things but their work. I'd clean them out with a besom if I had my way. So long as Sir William takes their counsel, we can look for no better success than what we've had. The General's slothful enough, God knows, without—"

"Aye, aye, to be sure," interrupted Hammond hastily. "So you'd sweep poor Arthur out to starve! And what would his mother say to that?"

"You know her?" asked Serle.

"Who doesn't?"

"Here's our country's honor and profit at stake," exclaimed Serle, his face paling with anger, "and we must give thought to what such a woman may say!"

"A remarkable woman." Hammond tilted his chair back on its rear legs and rocked to and fro in a way that made Gaine fear for it. "Mischievous too, and powerful. If I were you, Serle, I'd keep my hand from Arthur Blythe."

"Have no fear," replied Serle bitterly. "I've served too long in diplomacy to attempt the impossible. I merely talk of it. Captain Blythe's beyond my reach, for all that he's only a poor cast-off of London fashion."

"He might have been more than that," said Hammond thoughtfully. "You know his story, I'm sure."

"As much of it as I choose to know. He was a rake and a gamester. Now he holds His Majesty's commission."

"The tale may amuse our host here," Hammond went on. "There's little to say of Blythe's sire—only that he was the son and grandson of rich attorneys and a gallant spender of the gold they'd cozened from the public. A port drinker, he was, and played faro at Almack's. His father mated him above his quality."

"To Stourbridge's youngest daughter," Serle put in, frowning. "She was a toast in my time, and rarely pretty. The old Marquess, her father, was drowning in debt and the settlement saved his estates."

"She was more than a beauty, my friend. She had wit as well, and a marvelous, subtle skill in the art of pleasing men. Once she was safely wed, she made the world of fashion her battleground. Old Fritz of Prussia never fought a campaign more cunningly than she did. 'Every woman's a rake at heart,' so says Mr. Pope, and she bore

out his words with a vengeance. Yet a rake must pay the
piper at last, whilst she never had a *liaison* that didn't
profit her. 'Twas prodigious. With each new keeper, she
raised up her family in social rank. Her husband, poor
wretch, was delighted with his bargain; she put horns on
his head but she had him made a Viscount. And as she
broke none of the forms of polite behavior, she kept free
of common scandal."

"Eh, sirs!" cried Gaine who had been listening open-
mouthed. "This was a wife, indeed!"

"There was some talk of her, though," said Serle.
"They say she was auctioned off once by one of her
lovers and brought eight thousand pounds."

"And took a percentage of the money for herself,"
added Hammond, laughing. "I had that story from a
man at White's but I doubt it was true; there's a limit to
audacity. Ten years ago was her great time. Whenever
she drove out, she was squired by sparks on horseback;
she masqued in men's clothes at the Pantheon; she
shone at a dozen country houses. Horry Walpole hated
her and wrote squibs about her, but ladies of the highest
ton were among her particular friends. Egad, gentlemen, there was something admirable about it all! Next
to her own comfort and convenience, she thought of
nothing but her family's preferment. The heir, her
elder son, turned out as silly as his father, so she fixed all
her pride and hope on Arthur. Her influence could have
brought him anything—money, a great match, political
place—anything, for he'd much of her brilliance in him.
You'll find verses of his in the *Foundling Hospital for
Wit,* as tasteful as any in it; the best judges admired

them. But he threw away all his chances after his first season. 'Twas almost perverse, the way he thwarted his mother's plans."

"Perhaps he chose to rise in his own way," said John, as the others stared at him in surprise. "Perhaps he misliked hers."

"He took a curious way then," Serle commented drily. "We draw nice distinctions in dissipation, my lad. He made all London talk of his follies but the talk was not to his credit. I despise the lady Viscountess, his mother, as I despise all calculating females of no honor —but I grant her a masterful will and a certain style. Whereas her son achieved nothing but a vulgar notoriety, and has come to nothing."

"The theater did for him at last," said Hammond. "He wouldn't be weaned from it, so they bought him a commission and bade him godspeed."

"The theater was his ruin?" asked Gaine. "I'd thought that the theater was in good esteem."

"He chose the wrong side of the curtain," Hammond explained. " 'Tis one thing, you must know, to lounge in a box and to visit the greenroom; 'tis quite another to live on terms of equality with players and theater poets. His mother gave him over when he sank that low. She cast him loose, and yet if she had a heart she'd have broken it over him."

John dined twice with Blythe in the week that followed; once again at Lenox's, and at Grant's tavern near the fort. The Captain refused John's offers to pay a share of the reckoning, saying with apparent sincerity that he was repaid in having so polite and knowing a companion. He was equally considerate when they went together to visit the theater, making John known to Captain DeLancey and others there who were painting the scenery for the forthcoming performance of *Tom Thumb,* and indeed embarrassing him by the complimentary style of his introductions. If there were something of proprietorship in Blythe's manner, a taking of credit for the discovery of a freakish, learned shopman, John gratefully overlooked it.

Blythe seemed another man in the shabby, red-painted, little building in John Street near the Broadway. He threw himself into the work of the theater with a boy's enthusiasm and a master's knowledge, rallying the actors with ready humor and directing them with tireless patience. He had completed three acts of a tragedy on the subject of Oliver Cromwell, he told John, and had composed the remaining two acts in rough draft. It was not fit as yet for a critic's eye, but so soon as he was satisfied with it he meant to beg the favor of John's opinion.

His mood was otherwise in the evenings, especially when he was in wine. He talked then with a wild and cynical freedom, exposing his views of mankind without scruple or pity.

"Either man preys, or he's preyed upon," he said. "Go where you will, 'tis ever the same—even in this trans-Atlantic Arcadia. Who dispenses favor at our headquarters? Why, who but our General's fair Sultana, Mistress Bet Loring, late of Massachusetts and now the Juno of the Province Arms! Her reign may end sooner than she thinks, poor wretch, for there's talk of some new attachment on Sir William's part—and she's no worse, to be sure, than any other lucky slut who battens on a man in power. Besides, her spoils are a fleabite compared with what our quartermasters and commissaries thieve from the King's treasury. The King of England, sir, is the most plundered gull in his own dominions. The fleet is short of rations, and how can it be otherwise when half of what's ordered never gets to the ships. The horses and wagons for our campaign in Jersey were hired from loyal Long Island farmers, along with the black slaves to drive 'em. Will they ever be returned or paid for, think you? Not in this world. The King will pay, of course, but the money will stick to some commissary's fingers and the gear itself will be sold again or lost. The King pays for houses already sequestered as spoils of war, for rum that the sailors never drink, for mythical flour and phantom cattle. He pays thrice over for every chaldron of coals and wagon-load of wood, for every truss of hay and yard of canvas."

"This starch fellow Serle," the Captain remarked on another occasion, "aye, and his ally, the worthy Doctor Inglis—what game do they play? What do they hope to achieve with their *Gazette?* They boast of our victories, yet any child can see that we're held fast in Jersey by an army of scarecrows. We met with a check near Princeton yesterday but Master Serle will labor it into a triumph. 'Rise up!' he bid the King's friends. 'Exert your power against the rebel despots and their deluded followers. England expects it; all England watches you.' No such thing. 'Tis all stuff and fustian. These broils in America mean little to any Englishman at home; they're an inconvenience, the loss of one market out of many, another blunder of an incompetent Ministry. So long as he has sufficient entertainment and belly-cheer, an Englishman watches nothing beyond the tip of his nose and expects nothing save money or place or power for himself. Your Serle is a fool if he believes his own heroics and a liar if he doesn't."

Oliver Higgins was pleased to hear of such talk. Blythe had let fall but little specific intelligence as yet —only that Admiral Lord Howe had taken to his bed with a bilious colic, and that British cruisers had gone on permanent station off the Delaware capes—but the tailor begged John to improve his opportunity in every way short of arousing suspicion. An aide at enemy headquarters who was so free of speech and so devoted to the bottle could not help but reveal some matters of importance.

"We've set you a hard task," he told John as they walked together up Broad Street, ostensibly on an errand of business. "And to think you must bear with Hugh Gaine's crotchets as well! No wonder you've a downcast look."

Higgins was mistaken in his judgment of the reason for John's lack of spirits. The irksome nature of his daily work and the strain of playing a part troubled him far less than his conscience did. He made no scruple of spying on men like Serle and Inglis, but it came hard to betray the confidence of Blythe who had declared himself a friend and who had exerted an influence on John's thinking out of all proportion to the time they had spent together. The Captain was a thorough Epicurean in his method of life, a skeptic of skeptics, and a scoffer at authority; yet he was also a wit, a lover of literature, and a man full of unexpected kindness and generosity.

His example had prompted John to an examination of almost every idea and motive which he had been taught to cherish. Why should any rational man concern himself with the condition of mankind in general, since most men and women were individually selfish, corrupt, and unworthy of trust? A thoughtful man should consider himself first of all, and thereafter only those few persons whom he discovered to be either necessary to his happiness or truly deserving of his regard. Conscience, honor, duty—the building stones of the social arch— might well be delusions, mere dame-school maxims, which a man of experience should discard when they ceased to profit him, or else exploit in his dealings with lesser and simpler folk. Alison Cunningham's conduct no longer seemed extraordinary when it was viewed in this perspective. It was what he should have expected; it was the norm, the way of the world. In time, the American cause might prove to be the greatest delusion of all.

These new lights of the mind possessed a luster in Blythe's presence which they lost in the silence and chill of Gaine's attic. John's memory held too many witnesses against their truth. Even if the gratification of self were the true end of the good life, the term had a wider extension than Blythe had given it. Some men might find gratification in money and power; John's father had found it in the gratitude of his poor patients. His brother Richard had found it in a fiery and thankless loyalty to the king. John Morgan was happy in his ceaseless struggle against official stupidity and indifference. And even Ambrose Serle, tight-buttoned functionary though he was, appeared to take comfort and pleasure from the coincidence of his work and his convictions.

Blythe himself had provided a capital argument against his own philosophy at their first meeting, when he had remarked how any man of sensibility tended to become a looker-on at life. Was this not equally true of one who consulted no other motive for action than his own immediate pleasure? John had broken free from an earlier snare of the will, which had been pride; he would not risk a second entrapment. Moreover, he sensed a hollowness at times in his new friend's professions, as if the bravado and brilliance were only a mask, or an armor against hurt—a revulsion against his mother and the society which had made her what she was.

They sat together in the Captain's quarters on the night of January 9th, in what had been the drawing-room of Isaac Roosevelt's house. An ample fire of coals burned in the grate and it was easy to forget the dry and piercing cold outside. Their dinner had been sent in from the tavern nearby and a bottle stood open between them, but Blythe seemed lost in his own thoughts and applied himself neither to the one nor the other.

"The *Gazette* says that we lost twenty men at Princeton," he said abruptly. " 'Tis a lie. We lost nigh on three hundred in that affair; my own regiment was a principal sufferer. The whole of Jersey's risen up against us. Our forage parties are ambushed and driven off. Yet the General amuses himself as if nothing's happened. What would you have? 'Tis winter. No civilized people fights in winter." He turned his deepset eyes on John. "Your glass is empty," he remarked, reaching out his hand and filling both John's glass and his own. "I must give you a hospitable example—and a toast. To England! To our country—a goddess in victory, an imbecile in defeat!"

" 'Tis only a few skirmishes lost," protested John, cautious as ever in his responses. "The General will make all right in the spring."

"I applaud your faith in Sir William Howe," said Blythe, regarding him with an ironical smile. "I would I could share it. Unhappily, I'm persuaded otherwise. We shall lose this war. Not this year, perhaps, or the year after, but we shall lose it. It isn't just a matter of Carleton failing to move from Canada, or the loss of a few brigades. We fight here without heart." He set his glass down on the table; his hand wavered toward the bottle, and then withdrew itself.

"You are ignorant of the world, my friend," he continued after a moment's silence. "I must instruct you." The affectation of cynicism remained in his tone and in the assumed ease of his pose, for he had thrown himself back in his chair and spoke with an exaggerated drawl; yet John had known the man long enough to know his moods and he was sure that this would be no trivial revelation.

"You must understand that there's not one England, but two," the Captain went on. "All the world knows the first of them, the outward England of the Court and the great county magnates, of the squires and the City merchants. 'Tis a bustling, brave, assertive country, and the nobles and gentlemen of England rule it as they have for many years past. And so they should, for they've made it with their own strong hands and their supple minds, whilst the other England of yeomen and mechanics and shopkeepers obediently served them. So long as the gentlemen justified their privileges by success and a reasonable degree of just dealing, the common sort were content. But they're a tough and enduring folk, those unknown people who do the work and fight the battles. Let the master's hand only falter and they're restive; let him drop the rein and they'll throw him. The hand of the master is faltering now, for the old blood's running thin. Sir George or Lord Edward lies snug in his hall and his lady never misses the season in town, but his factor goes about the estates like a damned usurer and wrings the last farthing out of the land. Look out the hall windows, out beyond the trim-cut trees and the tidy lawns; misery lies there! Hunger gnaws at the people of the village, ploughing their few stony acres with starved cattle. They won't be patient forever. Neither will the people in the new factory cities, from the iron-master down to his grimiest puddler. And when they rise, we shall go. I pray it be after my time, although there's justice in it. My own ancestors were hard-fisted rascals who laid a whole county under contribution, yet they helped make England great—and what am I by comparison!"

"You look for a rebellion at home?" asked John, astonished.

"My dear fellow, I look for nothing but my own ease and pleasure," replied Blythe with a return of his usual manner. "But I'd have you know that these restive, mechanical creatures at home are all friends to the rebel cause—so spare me any further prophesies of Sir William's success. Even should he win a few battles, it will not matter. If America can hold the sympathy of common Englishmen, as she now has it, she must be victorious in the end—be it in two years or ten or fifty."

"You don't appear distressed by the prospect."

"Ah, but I am," returned Blythe, filling a glass and draining it. "I'm distressed for posterity—for all those unfortunates who'll never know the joys of privilege as I've known them. My grandfather's chaplain sat below the salt and never dared wait for the dessert, but his successor reproves my cousin to his face. This, as the philosophers say, is progress. Those fine, gay gentlemen in the Commons House who make nothing of slipping a bribe or two under their ruffles will give place to black-coated chuffs neither fine nor gay—but will the knavery cease? Nay, sir, it will not; but a manner of life will pass. What think you of this for a day's diversion? To get up at ten from bed with never a care in the world; to lounge about until noon in dressing gown and slippers, conning over a playbook or the latest poem, sipping chocolate, playing with the spaniel. And then to Wattier's or White's for cards, no matter if you win or lose. After dinner, you're off on a ramble through the town with a pair of stout chairmen to back you in a brawl if need be, and you fall into bed as the watch cries three. You've elbowed your way into the puppet show, perhaps; or you've called at the Opera to see the latest Italian singers; or you've only stood still in the street to watch the lovely, languid ladies looking out from their carriages and sedan-chairs—none of your high-colored, rustic hoydens such as pass for ladies here. There's Vauxhall, if you're in the humor for an adventure in the dark walks; or Ranelagh and tea, and a comfortable seat in a box whilst you ogle the pretty girls making a round of the room. And there's always the theater, bless it—both the patent houses, and poor Sam Foote's, and the minor houses right down to the tawdriest booth at Sadlers Wells."

He was all animation as he spoke, as if even the thought of London roused his spirits.

"I think I might tire of such a life," said John. "It lacks a purpose. It might even lack novelty after a time."

"Never. Not so long as you drew breath. Each day there's a new sensation to talk of—be it another Junius come to judgment, or ranting Jack Wilkes, or a contest of wits in Parliament, or only a tale of a Countess and her footman. And when all the gossip and tattle palls, there's another society for a man of taste—the company of the poets and the players. What's better than a chair at the Turk's Head or at the Mitre, to hear Sam Johnson, the dictionary-maker, in his downright vein? Or Goldsmith, the Irish genius, merry in his cups? Or a dozen other whimsical fellows spinning out malice and satire 'til the candles gutter. Nay, sir, as Johnson himself once said, 'A man who is tired of London is tired of life.' "

His youthful ambition to study at Edinburgh and to walk the hospitals there and in London was much in John's thoughts as he hurried home to Hanover Square. He had long since schooled himself to shun the topic, since nothing was to be gained by brooding over his mother's mean frustration of his hopes, but Blythe's talk had revived it. His recent experience must have strengthened him in stoicism, for he found to his surprise that the disappointment no longer pained him. He had missed his chance to learn from great men of his profession but that was all. He could never have known the life which Blythe had described so enthusiastically, or rather elegized; he could only have looked on at it from the outside, like a child staring at the goods in a pastry-cook's window. And was it not better to share in the making of a new society than to attend, a stranger and unwanted, at the deathwatch of the old?

Next day after dinner, Gaine showed himself unusually familiar as they sat at table in the upstairs room. He sent the maidservant for a bottle of spirits and brewed up a punch, pressing a glass on John and taking the better part of the bowl for his own portion.

"Ye've observed, I'm sure, that I'm somewhat strict in my notions of morality," he began when the servant had gone and the door was closed. "I'd a father and mother who taught me to tell truth, and I've honored their teaching all my life—all my life, lad, barring a wee fall from grace now and then in business matters. And that's what makes my present condition hard. I say it with sorrow, but I must say it—the King's people here in New York treat truth like a drab. Master Serle and his friends have filled the *Gazette* with vaunting and lies. My conscience is woe for what they've done."

"They're doing their duty as they see it, sir."

"So they are, so they are," exclaimed Gaine. "And God forbid that I do aught to let them in their duty. But my name's printed on that paper. 'Tis Gaine's *Gazette* in all men's eyes, and the lies will be fathered on me."

"What matter? You'll have the credit for your loyalty. Perchance, the King may hear of it."

"Aye, that's true. So I shall." The printer's face creased with worry, with the struggle between his need to tell his doubts to someone and his prudent urge to conceal them. He leaned over toward John and dropped his voice almost to a whisper. "But what if the royal cause should fail? What then?"

"Come August, there won't be a single rebel in arms," John answered confidently.

"I pray you may be right." Gaine appeared to take a moment's comfort in the thought and then looked anxious again. "But even so, we shan't see an end of trouble. The harm that's been done here will take an age to repair. We were used to honest trade in New York before these thieving commissaries and quartermasters came with their sly tricks and their hands held out for vails. And that's no the worst of it. There's the catchett, as the vulgar call it, that Governor Tryon devised to ruin the credit of Congress. 'Tis a good enough scheme for his present purpose, but what's to keep his clever fellows from carrying on the business after there's peace?"

"Catchett?"

"Counterfeit Congress money and state bills of credit. 'Tis so well forged, it fools the rebels themselves. Thomas Cumings at the Coffee House has charge of it, and any trusty man who'll undertake to smuggle it out to the King's friends in Connecticut may have it of him by the bale. Thereafter, it's scattered all over the country. The Loyalists use it to pay the rebel taxes." The ghost of a smile crossed his lips at the thought. "Nonetheless, it's a bad business," he went on. "I've no scruple at all about bilking the Congress, but the false money's used in trade, so they say, and that's a serious matter."

"Is it printed here, did you say?"

"I didn't say," replied Gaine sharply, too late aware of his indiscretion. "I know naught of it beyond what I hear."

Two hours later, John knocked at the back door of the tailor's house and was admitted by the master himself. The workmen and the servants had all departed, so Higgins led the way upstairs to his small sitting-room where a kettle was steaming on the hob. Glasses in hand, they were soon in talk.

"This is excellent," said Higgins, looking up from the two smudged slips of paper which John had given him. "A schedule of the return of sick from each of their regiments, and a list of the forces assigned to foraging duty. Can we trust them?"

"They were set up on Gaine's press and the copies delivered to Howe's headquarters. What you have there are proofs; the pressman crumpled them and dropped them on the floor. However, I've more news—and of greater importance, I think—"

"Better and better," exclaimed the tailor after John had informed him of the false money and the means by which it was circulated. "So Thomas Cumings is the man and the Coffee House the place! I'm acquainted with Cumings; he's an officer in Wentworth's Tory regiment. Rely on it, we'll keep close watch on all who visit him and lay them by the heels if they seek to cross Westchester. 'Tis pity Hugh didn't say where they print the counterfeit."

"Not on his own presses, else I'd have seen or heard of it."

"They have presses aboard their ships-of-war. They may even print the bills in London. But that's of lesser import now that we can nab the carriers and discover their agents in Connecticut. You've done your country a service, Frayne. The General will have this news before tomorrow's sunset."

"I marvel at your assurance," said John as he rose to go. "The British keep a strict guard on the roads."

"Not so strict as they think it. We've a number of ways to deceive them."

"Of which you'll tell me nothing," John remarked with some irony.

"'Tis not for lack of trust in you," said Higgins. "Some day I'll tell you all our secrets gladly, but the fewer who know them now the better for the cause."

CHAPTER NINE

ON THE Sabbath day following, which was the twelfth day of January, John set forth early on a solitary walk beyond the Collect pond and then westward to the shore of the Hudson. The day was fine but very cold; the sun glistened on immense floes of ice which had drifted down from the upper parts of the river and were grinding dangerously against the hulls of the ships at anchor. He could see a group of seamen standing by the capstan of the vessel nearest inshore, and others in the shrouds and manning the yards preparatory to a change of station.

If the floating ice were a menace to ships-of-the-line, perhaps it might also embarrass the traffic of sloops and pettiaugers between the city wharves and the British posts in Jersey. Since the battle at Princeton, the enemy had drawn his forces back to the immediate neighborhood of Brunswick, Amboy and Paulus Hook, but the Jersey farmers made little of the risks involved in bringing their livestock and hoarded grain to market at those places. King George's gold outweighed both their fears and their scruples. Beyond the British lines, all hither

138

Jersey was a no-man's land—the prey of outlaws and forage parties, the scene of a desperate *petite guerre* between Tory volunteers and patriot militiamen. Night raids on isolated farmhouses, ambushes along the roads, plunder, rapine and murder were become commonplace in that seeming placid country across the river. Daily, the Provost prison or the Bridewell or one of the sugar houses received new levies of woebegone creatures taken in Jersey or on Long Island. Recruitment of the Tory raider battalions was no hard task. Many of the Jersey and Westchester Loyalists who had thronged into the city for fear of the Whig militia were now destitute and living on a meager British allowance of food. Animated by need and by hatred of their sometime neighbors, they were only too happy to join a Tory "Greencoat" company and strike back.

As John walked southward along the riverside, he came in view of the King's College building and was reminded of John Morgan. This much was certain, he thought, with respect to the director of hospitals— wherever the fortunes of war had carried that small but mighty man he was still courageous, still chafing under the yoke of ignorant authority, still sanguine of ultimate success. John envied him that habit of mind which prompted him to struggle against difficulties rather than reason about them. It was a fortunate trait which he himself lacked to his hurt.

The College building had suffered little change. The British occupied it as a hospital for their own sick and it looked neat and well-tended; the windows shone in the sunlight and smoke was rising from the chimneys. No such cheerful sight was to be seen eastward at the Common, where the gray stone walls of the Provost and the Bridewell stood grim amidst a clutter of wooden bar- racks. Countless Americans wasted therein, desperate, starving and cold. The inhumanities he had himself ex- perienced while a prisoner were trifling in comparison with what the captured men now suffered. Even Hugh Gaine had come reluctantly to credit the tales told in the city of the Provost-Marshal's cruelty to his charges— the scourgings and hunger, the deprivation of water, fire and blankets, the gallows on the little hill to the north which seldom lacked for a ghastly occupant.

Since he could do nothing to help the prisoners, John strove to put their plight from his mind. A few late- comers were entering St. Paul's Chapel as he passed be- low it on the river road. Service had already begun; he heard the voices of the congregation raised in a response before the doors were closed again. An alien church it was, and an alien creed which he could not accept, yet he felt moved to join in its worship on this shining Sab- bath morning. This was not a common impulse with him; he had felt so last on the evening of Concord fight when he had come upon the bodies of his slain towns- men and had tried to find reason in why they died. He had prayed then in his own way and he wished he might pray now. But as he stood and pondered the matter, he was minded of Sabbath days at Wendham—of Parson Havens furious in the pulpit; of his mother's scorn of her lowly seating; of his brother Richard's voice in the choir; of Squire Cunningham, Alison's father, swelling like a peacock in the foremost pew. The impulse of the spirit was lost in a flow of memories, some grave and others lightsome but all of a peculiar poignancy since they had life now only in his mind; they were past, they were gone, they were dreams.

He passed the great forage yard near the ferry to Paulus Hook and turned up Cortlandt Street. When he reached the Broadway, he found it lively with church-goers and mere strollers—merchants bewigged and be-cloaked, British soldiers in red coats and Hessians in blue or black, children begging for pennies, noisy sailors from the King's ships, artisans in frieze or homespun with their wives clinging to their arms. At Wall Street, he stood aside to allow a gaggle of women to pass, all in wide, embroidered skirts, all jabbering in German.

When he came at last to Hanover Square, Gaine's crabbed maidservant opened the door to his knock. "Master's at church," she told him. "Breakfast's over. Here's a writing for ye that a soldier brought—and a saucy blackguard he was, to be sure."

The note was from Blythe. "Make yourself as fine as you can," John read. "I shall come for you tonight at seven and make you known to a choice company."

Shortly before the appointed hour, John gave up all hope of making a genteel appearance. He had polished his boots and attempted to dress his wig, but his coarse coat was shabby beyond his skill to furbish it. The mys-terious company to which Blythe had bid him must make the best of him as he stood. He had never sought to excel in dress and he did not propose to be fazed now by any lack of fashion.

The Captain was punctual, for a wonder. Preceded by a man with a torch, they set off up Wall Street and north along Nassau Street. As they walked, Blythe told John something of the character of the entertainment which they would receive, and also of Mrs. Forbes, their hostess. Before her marriage to Major Henry Forbes, she had dazzled the *ton* in London as the only daughter of a rich Wiltshire baronet, a man of vast pretensions and ambition. Blythe had known her as a modish young woman, a little *passée* but still much admired, and he had wondered like everyone else in the great world at her choice of a husband. Major Forbes was a gentleman neither gifted nor wealthy, and in nothing resembled the kind of match to which she and her father had aspired. He had risen no further in the army, nor was he likely to, and the lady's ambition had become of necessity circumscribed. All that she had was a sufficiency of money and a thirst for revenge on a world that had used her ill, as she thought. Having followed her husband dutifully to America, she consoled herself as best she could, whilst he, poor dupe, was serving with troops in the field. "And yet I shouldn't scoff at her," said Blythe in conclusion. "Let her motives be what they may, she provides us a taste of refinement in this provincial desert. Mind you don't take a hand at cards," he warned. "If your luck is good, they'll rook you; if it's bad, they'll fleece you. Ah, here we are."

They had halted before a house on Beekman Street just off Nassau—a handsome brick structure of three stories, its windows ornamented with flat arches, its door opening between Greek columns.

A servant in livery admitted them to a wide entrance hall, helped them put off their hats and cloaks, and brushed the mire from their boots.

The long room or parlor on the left was well filled with company, gentlemen for the most part and about equally divided between soldiers and civilians; the voices of the few ladies present shrilled above the hum of talk and laughter. Across the hall in a smaller drawing room, the card-players were already busy. At first sight the house bespoke comfort and indeed elegance. The floors were polished to a high gloss, as was also the staircase of mahogany wood that rose in a graceful curve to the apartments on the second floor.

"My dear Blythe!" exclaimed a lady in a powdered and plumed head-dress who came over to him and took both his hands within her own. "You do me too much honor."

"No honor can be too great for Mrs. Forbes," he answered, bowing.

"And that, to be sure, explains why you haven't called on me this fortnight," she said, looking past him at John. "Pray present this gentleman to me."

"My friend, Master Absalom Prentiss—an unfortunate scholar and a vastly sensible man."

She wore a hoop petticoat with an overdress of lilac silk heavily embroidered; her only jewel was a necklace of opals and diamonds in a gold setting. Her pale face was of a heart-shape, its pallor accentuated by her full, pouting lips which were painted a bright crimson. But neither her face, nor her opulent figure, half-hid and half-revealed beneath a deep collar or scarf of lawn, attracted John's interest so much as the great black eyes with which she studied him. They were at once lustrous and cold, inviting and repellent.

"Had you not come here with Captain Blythe," she said, acknowledging John's bow with a mere nod, "I'd have taken you for a shopman."

"And so he is," replied Blythe equably. "A learned shopman to earn his bread, a friend to the Muses in his leisure. And as I've claimed him for a friend, dear lady, we'll say no more of it."

"You're an insolent fellow, Blythe," the lady remarked, still gazing at John. "Yet you were ever so, and I must remember that these are levelling times. Master Prentiss," she went on, "as you are here, and so politely recommended, I bid you welcome. I ask no more of my guests than genteel manners and a little wit."

"I can promise you neither, madame," answered John, not at all liking the position in which he found himself. "You must take me as I am."

Once again she surveyed him from top to toe, and then she smiled—the briefest mocking curl of her bright lips. With a curtsey, first to him and then to Blythe, she turned away and rejoined the company.

"You've caught her fancy," said Blythe, taking John by the arm and leading him into the long room. "I know her ways. 'Twill bring you more ill luck than good. And now you must excuse me for a little whilst I play the politician and greet some acquaintances. They're not worth your notice, else I'd make you known to them. Speak to anyone you choose. There's no ceremony in this house."

John was content to walk about unnoticed and take stock of the rooms and their occupants. The furniture and other appointments were of the first quality. The walls of the long room were papered with scenes of the procession of the seasons and hung with a number of mirrors in gilt frames. The chairs were of mahogany or black-walnut wood and after Chippendale's designs;

some had haircloth seats, some were upholstered in blue damask as was also a large sofa. The windows were ornamented with drapes of a matching blue silk. Wall sconces and a chandelier of crystal lusters cast a brilliant light over all, and coals burning in grates beneath the carved mantels of two fireplaces threw out a pleasant warmth. At the rear of the long room, a dining-room opened out wherein two waiters presided over a large table and a smaller tea-table laden with dishes of sliced fowl and other delicacies. Bottles and decanters were ranked on a splendid mahogany sideboard.

The ladies, he observed, remained seated, each with her attendant circle of admirers; the gentlemen moved about from group to group, sometimes going to the tables to replenish their glasses or to fetch a lady's supper. Only the card-players, intent upon their business in the smaller room, were relatively quiet; the chatter in the long room was uninterrupted and almost boisterous.

John knew some of the guests by sight—George Clerk, the Barrack-Master and his intriguing wife; Captain Bryne of the *Andromeda* man-of-war; Samuel Bayard in the green uniform of his Tory volunteer regiment; the two Kemble brothers—but the company was composed in the main of redcoated officers and of the new people who had risen to affluence through the war. There were Commissaries and Deputy-Commissaries, speculating merchants and vendue-masters, clerks from the Navy Office and from the several commissariats, all in fine broadcloth and satin and ruffles, with bullion buttons on their waistcoats and silver buckles on their high-heeled shoes. Their women, whether wives or mistresses, were of the same adventurous type—their heads were

dressed in the fullest fashion with an amazement of
feathers, lace, and ornamental pins set in hair swept
high off the forehead; they wore gowns of the choicest
silks and *à la mode;* their satin shoes had pointed toes
and heels a good three inches high. Despite all their outward show, they were easily recognized for what they
were by a certain uneasy assurance of manner, a demand
for notice that masked the fear of a snub. Mrs. Bayard
looked unhappy amongst them, as if she were wishing
herself at home in the country at Greenwich, rather
than in company with Mrs. Clerk and Margaret Mon-
crieffe.

"Oh la, you creatures!" burst out a bouncing red-
haired girl who was surrounded by a group of officers. "I
vow I shan't sit here if you mean to be so wicked." But
she made no move to go.

"The Fuel Office is the best place," John overheard a
bilious-looking civilian say to his neighbor. "There's a
fortune in it. They cut the wood in Jersey on free
commons—no matter where, since some rebel's sure to
own it. It costs them nothing, and His Majesty buys it at
the market price in New York."

" 'Tis much the same with horses and horned cattle.
Cash in hand at the Commissary's office, and no questions asked."

"Aye, but the risk's greater—"

Everything was for sale in this city, thought John.
Honor, duty and love no less than plundered cattle and
stolen wood. And not here alone. He recalled his last
visit to his native place, in the winter before the fall of
Boston. The members of the Wendham Committee
were growing rich out of trade in confiscated Tory

properties. Avarice and opportunity had corrupted their earlier motives of patriotism. Or had aught ever moved them but the hope of gain?

"Odds life, if you're not a picture of gloom," said Blythe, returning from his tour of the rooms. "And no wonder. Saw you ever such a vulgar crew? And such women! Damme, if I understand why any woman is suffered to live beyond twenty-five; she's only in the way, and has too devilish good a conceit of herself to know it. *A propos,* let's pay our court to our hostess who sits like a Sibyl on the sofa yonder and watches us out of the corner of her eye. But first, let's fill our glasses."

Mrs. Forbes appeared to take no notice of them when they joined the group about her. She gave all her attention, as it seemed, to the gossip which her swains had each at his tongue's end—tales of *liaisons* made and broken, of knaveries petty and great, of egotism, greed and triumphant malice. The talk turned at last on the plight of the Loyalists.

"They come to me to complain of their rations," announced a paunchy fellow who was chief clerk to General Robertson, the commandant of the city. "Not a man-jack but would have me believe that he'd lost a fortune in the King's cause. I tell 'em that no one's to be favored, but do they take my meaning? Nay, they're that dull and ungrateful they don't even hint at an accommodation. Egad, I must live as well as they."

" 'Twas the same in London," added a staff captain. "They sit all day in the Coffee House on Threadneedle Street, scribbling addresses and memorials for compensation of their losses, but they never think to give a *douceur* in the right places. Don't they know how the

world wags? Yet they're the fortunate ones who've a
pound or two in pocket and they could well afford it.
You should see the ragtag who shuffle up to the Treasury Office for bread money—the ones who have nothing,
and never did have, I'll be bound!"

And one is my brother Richard, thought John.

"Nay now, let's talk of something gayer," put in an
officer whom John had seen now and then at Higgins's
shop. "The new Sultana, shall it be?"

" 'Tis only a tale," sneered Robertson's clerk. "Mrs.
Loring has the General fast in her toils."

"I'll give three-to-one that he casts her before Shrove
Tuesday."

"Fair odds, but a poor bet," said Mrs. Forbes. "If the
minx is but half what the gossips report of her, poor
Loring is as good as cast right now."

"Is the girl in the city?" asked Blythe.

"She's expected daily. Sir William set eyes on her first
in Halifax, since when he's intrigued mightily to get her
to New York. She's from Boston like the Loring—a
refugee's daughter. And a coy creature, so they say."

The words rang in John's ears like a passing-bell.
Alison had fled to Halifax. But surely a hundred others
had done so, too.

"A coy creature?" repeated Blythe. "Never. If there's
one thing predictable of our commander-in-chief, it's his
taste in women. I'll limn this girl for you. A loud,
buxom, red-cheeked wanton, with hair like flax and the
manners of a milkmaid. Believe me, if there's to be a
new Sultana, that's what she'll resemble."

"We verge on treason, gentlemen," said Mrs. Forbes,
rising from the sofa. " 'Tis no light matter to question

Sir William's taste. Master Prentiss, lend me your arm and take me away from these dangerous men."

It was an obvious device, for after a single turn about the room she seated herself again and made John sit beside her.

"And were you indeed born and reared in this wilderness?" she asked, after they had talked a little on indifferent subjects. "I can hardly credit it."

"Should I please you better in war-paint, with a hatchet in my hand?"

"Nay, I'm not such a fool as that. Yet I've found so many clowns here in broadcloth and silk that I'm amazed to discover a gentleman in homespun."

"You must enlarge your experience of Americans," he replied.

"I should like nothing better."

It seemed to John that her words meant more than a polite assent, and that she had intended it so. Her eyes shone in her pale face and the set of her painted mouth softened; she looked at once younger and more kind.

"Will you undertake to instruct me?" she went on. "Prejudice is so vulgar, and you could help me rid myself of it. I shall be at home to you whenever you call."

Before he could frame a proper reply, her expression altered and she turned from him abruptly to greet a newly arrived guest—a slim exquisite who had been standing nearby and awaiting her notice.

"Drummond, dear friend," she cried, giving him both her hands as she'd done with Blythe. "I'd thought you were still in London."

" 'Twas a desert without you," he answered, seating himself without ceremony in the place from which John had risen. "All your friends languish. I bring you their sighs and tears."

Accepting his dismissal, John sought out Blythe and found him in play at one of the card-tables.

"I give good counsel but I rarely take it," the captain said. "Go home, if you must. As for myself, I'll stay and woo fortune."

John made his way back in the dark to Hanover Square in a mood of almost boyish excitement. The men and women he had seen at Mrs. Forbes's house were a loose and inferior society but they observed at least the outward forms of politeness and he was grateful for any respite, even for a single evening, from the monotony of Gaine's household. Moreover, his hostess's interest in him was as provocative as it had been unexpected. She had left him in no doubt of her preference and in little doubt of what she wished of him. Such women did not invite the visits of a country schoolmaster for the improvement of their intellects, and if she had some motive other than whim he was careless of it. The prospect of dalliance with a woman of the world was an inviting one after the disappointments and frustrations he had known during the two years past. He had no duty to any other woman, no sworn word to keep, and he was satisfied from Blythe's account of Mrs. Forbes that she was practiced in such affairs. Her heart had survived other sieges and would survive this. To be sure, he would be no partner in a grand passion but rather a player in a small comedy—indeed, only an incident in the lady's revenge on mankind—yet what did it matter. It were time, perhaps, that he took a revenge of his own.

He lay wakeful a long time in his attic bed. The gossip about the new Sultana had moved him more than he had supposed was possible. He had striven with all his strength of mind to forget Alison Cunningham, yet he found himself with a concern for her that made mock of his efforts. Reason it as he would, he was disturbed by any trouble or shame that befell her; the bonds of sympathy, tied in old friendship and old love, were still unbroken. And yet, if she were indeed the new mistress, what a sour jest! What a pinch for the pride of the Honorable Stanhope Damer! That rakish dragoon who had taken Alison from him would have to play a new role—the cuckolded husband. And by his own commander-in-chief!

He was ashamed suddenly of his thoughts. Even if the talk were truly about Alison, she might have laid herself open to it unwittingly, perhaps to serve her father, perhaps even to further her husband's ambition. It would have been like her to push opportunity to the limit in currying favor with Sir William Howe, but she had too much delicacy, too much taste, to venture beyond what was fitting and lawful. He remembered her coming to meet him among the lilacs in her garden at Wendham, the night they had planned their escape together to Boston; he remembered that other time when she had pledged herself to him, and her mouth pressed against his, and the soft, low tone of her questioning voice: "Will you think of me always so—always like spring?" Aye, he would; he could not help it. All that had chanced had been his own fault, perhaps, for his breaking his promise to go with her to Boston.

The thought of Alison saddened him but it made him

think again and with less enthusiasm of a sentimental adventure with Mrs. Forbes. Such an intrigue might divert him and soothe his injured pride, yet it could prove a dangerous pastime. Her preference would cause endless tattle; he would become conspicuous; and this he could not risk. Master Absalom Prentiss, Tory schoolmaster and Gaine's drudge, was safe so long as he kept his humble station. His identity with John Frayne, escaped prisoner of war, might easily be discovered if he aroused the jealousy and malice of the people with whom she associated.

CHAPTER TEN

HE STOOD and waited for Mrs. Forbes's door to be opened to him, more fearful lest her encouragement had been only a freak than mindful of the risks he would run in acting upon it. Throughout the two days that had passed since Blythe had made him known to the lady, his fancy had rebelled against reason and rioted like an amorous boy's. A reckless and passionate sensuality possessed him; his loneliness and disappointments were for the moment absorbed in this unfamiliar emotion. Now her bold, dark eyes tempted him to folly; now it was the luxurious grace of her carriage and walk; now the soft flattery in her voice when she bade him come to her, a tone which had promised nothing and suggested everything.

On entering the house, he was disturbed to find a noisy company present, quite as numerous as on the night of his first visit. In his impatience and inexperience, he had not stopped to consider that this might be so, nor was his confidence restored by the lady's reception of him. Mrs. Forbes was seated on the sofa in the long room and greeted him, on his going up to her, with a cold, abstracted courtesy. She returned her attention almost at once to the men surrounding her, among whom John recognized Captain De Lancey and John McAdam, the Commissioner of Naval Prizes.

"You've called to press your advantage, I see," whispered Blythe, who appeared at his elbow as he turned away in some confusion. " 'Pon honor, I hadn't thought you were so combustible. 'Twill be an ill thing for you, my friend, but if you must, you must. Pay no heed to her present caprices; she was never the creature to yield at the first summons. Be patient and play your cards with a cool head. As I shall attempt to do in the small room yonder. I lost forty guineas there last Sunday night."

Mrs. Forbes proved as elusive as quicksilver, flashing in rose-colored silk from one group to another, never alone, and acknowledging John's presence as she passed him by no more than an affected and conventional smile. As the tall clock in the card-room struck nine, he had about determined to take his leave when she approached him and drew him out of the crowd to sit with her on a wooden bench in the hall.

"You were kind to come tonight," she said, "but we'll have little chance to talk or be friends. You see what a weary life I lead with these fine folk who care nothing for me. I vow I'm like the mistress of an inn."

"I was taught to think hospitality a virtue."

"Hospitality!" She laughed. "Nay, not at all. I care as little for them, but I must have company about me. I'd die of dullness without a clack of tongues and the feeling that I'm at the heart of affairs."

"I fear I'll be little to your mind then. We hear naught but petty gossip at Gaine's shop."

"Blythe says that you've sensibility. We women esteem it above all else."

"He's a friend and praises me too much. Yet I've enough of it to be sensible of you."

She drew back in mock amazement; then she smiled. As at their first meeting, her natural smile transformed her; years and experience dropped away from her and she was a novice again, and young and desirable.

"Ah, now you disappoint me," she said, "for you speak as anyone might."

"I speak as my heart prompts me. You fill my thoughts and I ask only to serve you."

"For ever and aye, I suppose," she replied, her look and tone at once affectionate and ironical.

"Only 'til you weary of me."

"How came you acquainted with Blythe?" she asked. "You're not of his kind. Perhaps you're other than you profess to be. Perhaps I should be wary of you."

It was only a random hit, he was certain, but it recalled to him the danger of the game he was playing.

"He took notice of me in the shop and was good enough to befriend me. I've no mystery about me, I do assure you. I'm only what I seem—a poor schoolmaster out of fortune, and your most humble servant."

"You're this much of a prodigy at least—that I've never before known Blythe to act with disinterest."

"Truly, you wrong him, and I—"

A burst of laughter from the long room interrupted John's speech and appeared to remind Mrs. Forbes of her duties as hostess.

"I must leave you now," she said, rising slowly from the bench and holding out her hand to him. "You're welcome to stay but I dare say you'd rather not. You have a man's freedom in such matters, whereas I must suffer fools gladly as all women must. Fare you well then. I shall have no company here tomorrow night."

Accompanied by the look she bent on him from under her long lashes, her words were unmistakable and he set off down Nassau Street in a mood of elation which stilled the small voices of caution and conscience.

The street was dark and deserted. The British patrols were enforcing the curfew strictly because of a rise in the number of robberies by night, so that John did not wait to be challenged when he saw a number of lighted lanterns bobbing towards him up Crown Street. He crossed over to meet the patrol, passing by the despoiled church on the southeast corner and halting before a tall building which adjoined the churchyard on the east—a gaunt structure five stories high, whose gray stone bulk showed forth no light save in the guard room beside the low, arched doorway. Here was an ill omen, he thought with sudden apprehension, for this was Livingston's sugar warehouse, now one of the city's most notorious prisons.

He gave his name to the officer commanding the patrol and handed over the pass which permitted him as Gaine's servant to go about the city at any time. While he waited for the pass to be read and returned to him, he stared idly up at a small, barred window, one of several which opened in the warehouse wall at about seven feet above the street level. The window was unglazed, presumably to admit air, and he took notice of it only

because the light of the lanterns fell on it and distinguished it from the others.

"Well enough," said the patrol officer, holding out
the pass to John. "Get along home with ye now—"

The patrol moved on. The lantern light no longer
illuminated the window, but in the brief interval when
it had, John had seen something that had banished all
thought of Mrs. Forbes from his mind. Two hands had
appeared of a sudden at the window, gripping the bars
as if the man within were straining desperately upward.
The hands soon relaxed their hold and were gone, yet
even in the dim light John had observed how thin and
corded they were, how eloquent of hopeless misery.

The footfalls of the patrol died away westward but
John continued to gaze at the darkened window. He had
passed by this building many times in recent weeks and
never without thought of its unhappy inmates, but not
until the sight of those pitiful hands had he felt so personal and awful a sympathy with them. Each detail of
his own imprisonment in the North Dutch Church renewed itself in his fancy with almost nauseating reality.
Although the Commissaries and their friends still lacked
for nothing, the British authorities were rationing food
and fuel for the townspeople and even for the garrison
troops. What privations must be visited upon the prisoners then, who had so little claim on British honor
and humanity! Bone-racking cold was their portion,
bread hard as flint or crawling-soft with weevils, fevers
and fluxes, and at last death like a kind comforter.
Whilst he, John Frayne, physician, ate well and slept
sound, ran mad after an English strumpet, and handed
on bits and shreds of intelligence that must be as useless

as they were trifling. How far had he fallen off, how much consulted his own ease and appetites! Blythe's fine-spun philosophy could no more gainsay this witness of human suffering than a spider's web could withstand the sweep of a serving-maid's broom. Conscience, bred in him by generations of self-judging, self-denying ancestors, could no longer be stifled by sophisms and he saw himself for what he had become. Remorse and disgust tormented him from within as fiercely as the storm-laden wind from the eastward stung his face. Forcing himself to action, he hurried off towards Hanover Square, leaning into the wind and struggling against each gust as if it were alive and an enemy.

From a window of his attic room, he peered out into the icy night. Snow was beginning to fall. The wind whirled it in a wild dance but soon it would lie still and white on the streets and rooftops of the city, disguising the filth and squalor on which it lay like the whitening of a sepulchre.

His first frenzy of self-reproach abated in time and gave place to resolution. He would return to the army; he would go to Higgins in the morning and demand to be smuggled out of the city. Under favor of Providence, he might hope to atone by faithful service for his sins of rash judgment since November. The thought of his hasty and ignorant condemnation of the General and the Congress was like ashes in his mouth. George Washington's failure at New York could well have been an effect of bad counsel by others; and they, in their turn, might have erred in perfect good faith. He had misjudged them all, as crassly as he had misjudged the poor creature Shawcross whose wits had been set wandering (as John was now fully persuaded) by all that he had seen and endured. The experience of the North Dutch Church, of Gaine's shop, of Blythe's drunken speeches, and of Mrs. Forbes's drawing-room had proved beyond dispute what he had known since Concord and should have clung to as the articles of his faith—that the errors, aye even the crimes, of his own people were naught as against what Britain stood for and practiced. Here at New York, he had observed a reflection in little of what Englishmen themselves must tolerate from their ruling class until, as Blythe had prophesied, they rose up in anger and burst their bonds. America's rebellion had sounded an alarm against degenerate Toryism every-where—the self-same Toryism that had sunk all Europe in poverty and ignorance, and would do the like injury to America unless it was confronted and defeated. As for the domestic rascals and their schemes, let the war be won first; justice would find them out in time.

The snow ceased falling at dawn but the skies were still clouded and big with another storm. John had thrown himself down to sleep in his clothes, but he slept only fitfully and was knocking at the tailor's door by seven o'clock.

Higgins received him with ill-concealed apprehension and took him at once to the street for their talk.

"You must be daft, coming here when my workmen are by," he complained as they walked together up Queen Street. "Don't come again without I summon you. And now what's amiss, for something is by the look of you."

"You're wrong, man, wrong and foolish," he protested after John had made his request and revealed his reasons for it. " 'Tis only a scruple. The news you've brought me has been of great value. And now that you're on such terms with Mistress Forbes—"

"I'll never go back to her. If I went to that house again, I'd spit in their faces."

"You must go back. You've a duty to go. Where else can a knowing eye and ear be better employed? We've no other agent so handsomely situated, yet you're ready to throw all over because you think it nobler to puke and give physick in the Jersey camp. Aye, that's where the army stands now. At Morristown. The General's taken up winter quarters there."

"Find means to send me there then," said John. "I've been meek and biddable long enough towards folk I should despise."

Higgins said nothing for a little and seemed to be weighing his next speech. They had passed the corner of Maiden Lane before he spoke.

"Since you're so dogged in this matter, I must tell you something I should not."

"Spare your conscience," answered John. "It will make no difference."

"I had this information only yesterday," Higgins continued, disregarding the interruption, "and on the highest authority."

"And through those mysterious channels which you've never seen fit to reveal to me?"

"True," said Higgins, without the least show of temper. "By one of my couriers. We stand at the turn of the tide. The French are ready to enter the war openly, and as our allies."

"Does that rejoice you?" demanded John. "Think you we'll fare any better under the papist French than under England's rule? It will be a long day before King Louis withdraws his foot should he once put it down on our land. Nay, if we must be puppets, let the strings be pulled from London."

"We must risk it, Frayne. We're too weak and divided to win this war of ourselves. The French power will tip the balance. Doctor Franklin says that they want nothing in return but our commerce and friendship. I've no opinion of this myself for I'm neither learned nor wise. Yet I'm willing to trust those who are."

"And what has this to do with me?"

They had halted near the head of Beekman's Slip, and all around them surged a noisy throng of merchants, clerks and runners.

"Everything," said Higgins, drawing John over by the wall of a hardware shop and out of the crowd. "If you persist in your present course, we've lost our best hope of learning what Howe means to do. Will he stay in New York? Will he march south and attack Philadelphia? Or will he ascend the Hudson to meet with the force that's poised to invade us from Canada? This is no matter to be talked of by subalterns or wharfingers. William Mooney's men shan't hear of it, nor I—but you might. You've the freedom of a house where secrets are whispered, where men brag in their cups and women chatter. In God's name, Frayne, only think of what turns on our having this knowledge! If the General could be certain of Howe's design, he'd move to check it with some chance of success. The French await only one great feat of our arms before they throw in with us, and this could be it. By the same token, a reverse will send them scampering."

"So that all is mine to make or to mar," replied John. It was ever so, he told himself bitterly; it was always he who was called on to yield his own will and purpose, and in such circumstances that a refusal would leave him as contemptible to himself as to others.

"Be patient only another fortnight," pleaded the tailor. "Improve your favor with the woman. Frequent her house. If you learn nothing in that time, I swear that I'll see you safe to Jersey."

CHAPTER ELEVEN

AFTER SOME further parley, John gave Higgins his reluctant promise to stay two weeks more in the city. He was convinced, despite the tailor's sanguine words, that no good would come of his consent, nor could. To suppose otherwise would be to suppose that Sir William Howe was a babbling fool, a character of the commander-in-chief which even his enemies would scruple to draw.

When John returned to Gaine's shop, he found a mass of proof sheets awaiting his eye—a solemn book of essays on military subjects by Major Donkin, and the forthcoming number of the *Gazette,* tricked out as usual with brag and lying inventions. Shortly before noon, a morning of tedious labor and of bickering with his master over trifles ended in a noisy quarrel when Gaine took offense at John's criticism of an advertisement in the newspaper.

"Would you teach me my own trade?" cried the master, pounding on his desk with his fist. "Let it stand, I tell ye—just as I writ it down."

"It's cram-full of untruth," retorted John. "Is it so

163

that you choose to appear before the public?" He snatched up the smudged and inky proof and began to read it aloud:

Leftenant Maynard of the garrison is perfectly cured by the use of Moredaunt's Drops of a most violent scorbutic. humor, attended with great loss of appetite and sleep. These Drops are to be had in square bottles from the only proprieter thereof in America— Hugh Gaine, printer and bookseller, at the Bible and Crown.

"I've Maynard's own statement to that effect," roared Gaine. "In his own proper hand."

"I'll find you a dozen hypochondriacal fellows who'll swear to any quack cure," John answered. "And what is your evidence for this?"

Moredaunt's Drops—he went on reading—*are an effectual cure for the leprosy, scurvy, fistulas and ulcers, bilious colic, rheumatism and gout. They will restore the most reduced constitution to perfect health in a very short time.*

"Have you proof that they won't?" demanded Gaine. "Would you have me cry bad fish?"

"All my witnesses are in Trinity churchyard," said John. "And as for what I'd have you do, I'd have you speak the truth in these matters."

"You're paid to keep shop and read proofs," cried the enraged Gaine, rising from his chair and wagging his forefinger in John's face. "Ye'll no tell me what's moral and what's not. I was a moral man ere you were born. Beseems, you've a tongue fitter for a lawyer than a dominie."

It had been a foolish thing to arouse his master's suspicions, and John regretted it now, just as he regretted his pledge to Higgins. Whereas he had gone last evening to visit Mrs. Forbes in a mood of high anticipation, he walked to her house now on leaden feet. This night, and for the two weeks to come, he must practice further deceit, a degrading and sordid masquerade, when he wished only to be free of the city and back with the army. The woman was a loose creature, to be sure, but she had treated him with kindness as Blythe had, and for this he must use and betray them both. The consciousness that he was performing his duty gave him but cold comfort, nor was he at all confident that he could support his part in the comedy. His sentimental passion for Mrs. Forbes had waned to indifference and he had never been given to cold sensualism. So accomplished an amorist as she must be would soon see through his pretense of lover.

The few persons abroad in the streets were soldiers and seamen, searching out a dram-shop if in funds, wandering restlessly if out of pocket. The civilians lay snug in the houses he passed, inhospitable, with closed shutters through whose chinks the light appeared. It kept very cold. There was no sign as yet of the January thaw.

When the man in livery announced him at the door of the long room, John was piqued at finding other company there—a merchant-looking fellow in a rich, new coat, three junior officers of the army, and General Robertson's fat clerk.

"You must sit here by me, Master Prentiss," the

hostess insisted after she had made John known to the others. "I doubt you'll be edified by our conversation, for these gentlemen have but one topic—Sir William Howe's new Dulcinea. She should be a second Helen, if she's to justify all that's said about her."

"She came ashore this morning," said Robertson's clerk importantly, "by boat from the *Gloucester* transport. One of my people was at the wharf and saw her."

"And was struck blind instantly by her beauty?" asked Mrs. Forbes, affecting a yawn. " 'Twould be a pretty story."

"Nay, ma'am, he had no more than a glimpse of her. She was whisked away in a carriage, no one knows where. Nor could he find out her name."

"I've heard her name said but I disremember it," put in the merchant. "She's a young girl, they do say, unmarried but vastly townish."

"Her nest should be well feathered by the time she quits it," remarked one of the officers. "Where the sex is concerned, our commander is only too generous. The Loring's husband is a rich man."

"And why should he not be?" asked Robertson's clerk with a snigger. " 'Tis all paid for from His Majesty's purse. Will she be listed under 'intelligence fees', think you? Or as 'travel expense, miscellaneous'?"

This gallant exchange was of singular comfort to John. "Unmarried," the merchant fellow had said, and he could not remember the girl's name. She could not be Alison then. Alison was Stanhope Damer's wife, and Damer was a man of sufficient mark for scandalous tongues to make much of his wife's frailty had such been the case. Determined as John was to be troubled no more by her memory, he was yet happy to acquit her of dishonor. As it often chanced when he thought of her, his imagination brought her suddenly and vividly present—this time, as she had looked in the summer of her sixteenth year, at the song-party in Jos Cushing's house at Wendham when he'd been first made acquainted with her. She had seemed like youth itself that day, so brave and lovely and unknowing, so foolishly hopeful of life.

"There's more than one such intrigue afoot," the merchant began with relish. "I had it of—"

"It must wait for another time, I fear," interrupted Mrs. Forbes, rising from her place beside John. "I've been happy in your company, gentlemen, but I pray you'll excuse me now. The Queen's birthday is three days hence, and I'll expect you and all my friends to sup with me that evening. But now my head aches sadly and you must go."

"I trust we've not been tedious, ma'am," said Robertson's clerk as the company took leave. "We're ever most sensible of your kindness—"

"Nay, sir, 'tis just as I said," she answered. "If you must find a subtler reason, blame it on your talk of Sir William's miss. All praise of female perfections gives me the vapors, unless I'm being complimented myself when I could listen all night. Pray tarry a little, my dear Prentiss. You told me once that you knew of a soothing draught; perchance, you'll compound it for me."

When the manservant had shut the door behind the last of her guests, Mrs. Forbes turned to John and led him back to the sofa in the long room.

"These gentry make me a habit," she said with a

laugh. "They're as constant in attendance here as bailiffs on a bankrupt. But all's well that ends well and we're private at last."

"For which I'm most grateful," answered John. "This day has seemed an age, for I live only in your sight."

"I vow I love such gallant falsehoods. But we've met for more serious matters, as you'll recall. Do you mean to begin my course of instruction at once?"

"I've thought better of it. To instruct so accomplished a lady would be an impertinence. Venus and the Graces would have their revenge of me."

"But truly, sir," she protested, "I'm wishful to learn all I can about your country. Why will you not believe me when I say it? Do you suppose that I've no more wit than I show at an evening rout? I'm no *bas bleu,* nor would I be one—but I'll take it ill if you think me a mere woman."

"I could never think that. Neither can I rest under your displeasure. So, then! Will you have me begin by bounding America on the four points of the compass? Or should I start with an account of the aborigines?"

"Enough, enough," she said, laughing and patting his hand. "No more of your wisdom and science. I find I've no head for them tonight. Let's talk of other matters— unless you're offended by my inconstant humor."

"You must think me quite ill-natured if you fear that I'd ruffle at your changing your mind."

"But I'm ever so, my dear Prentiss. I do change my mind, and often. No man can count on me. Does that disturb you?"

"If I'm admitted to your friendship, I'll study to remain your friend. Nothing will disturb me and I shall be the happiest of men."

" 'Tis such a cold word, friendship," she said with a little, affected shudder. "It minds me of old age and discretion."

"Yet it's often the first step towards indiscretion."

"Have you found it so?"

"Few men can stay discreet in the presence of conquering beauty."

"Lord, sir!" she exclaimed, leaning back against the cushions and giving him a long stare. "You show more than a prentice hand at work like this. I declare, my head's quite giddy with your politeness."

"As mine is with my admiration of you."

"Words are nothing," she murmured, closing her eyes. "I'm weary of words."

He seized both her hands and raised them to his lips. She did not oppose him.

How had he ever believed himself enamored of this woman, he thought, even as he kissed her hands! Only loneliness and frustration could have made him think that he was. Her eyes were brilliant, but they were over-knowing and heartless; the proud assurance of her manner was arrogance as he now observed it; her voice rang harsh. Even her body, displayed tonight to perfection in a *négligée* dress of silver damask sprigged with scarlet, seemed overblown and a prize too often bestowed to be worth the winning. Far from appearing desirable, she was the very type and symbol of all that he loathed in the society that had bred her. A weary disgust welled up in him. Let come what might, he could persist no longer in this counterfeit of emotion. She might think what she chose. Letting go her hands, he moved back and away from her.

Her eyes flew open, startled.

"Are you so faint-hearted then?" she asked in a languorous voice, misconceiving his action. "You were bold enough in your speech—" And then, studying his expression of face more closely, she read the truth in it.

"You're too nice for me, are you?" she cried, striking him across the mouth with all her strength. "How dare you play Joseph with me!"

"Would you rather I deceived you?"

"Save your shabby moralities for your low-bred American wenches," she answered, springing to her feet. "Have I lived to be scorned by a schoolmaster! And a clownish, American schoolmaster to boot! Yet I've only myself to blame for condescending. How else should I look to be served in a nation of bribe-takers, punks and cheats!"

"I assure you, madame," said John, growing angry himself, "your account of my countrymen is better given of your own."

"Was there ever an American who was a gentleman?" she cried in a fury. "Was there ever one who didn't have his price? You'll swear to anything for a fee, or to save your beggarly necks. Your women come crawling at the chink of a bag of guineas. Witness that slut, the Loring! Witness Sir William's new trull, who's as true-born a Yankee as ever sang psalms through her nose."

"You professed to know nothing of her, not half an hour ago."

"I said nothing of her, you fool, which is quite another thing. Will you have her story, chapter and verse? Then harken. She's lodged at Turtle Bay near the Beekman house where Sir William resides. She's a low, brown, slender thing who took his fancy at Halifax, whither she'd come with an old, cogging fellow she called her father. An officer of dragoons was her keeper then—one Damer, whom nobody liked. Some said he'd promised her marriage—"

She stopped short; the look on his face terrified her. Fearing lest he do her a mischief, she ran to the bell-pull and tugged at it. But John did not await the arrival of her servants. He was through the door in an instant and hastening down Nassau Street like a man pursued by fiends.

Stumbling and slipping along the icy streets, he wandered for a long time only barely conscious of his surroundings. He did not doubt that the woman had told the truth. The story had occurred to her in the heat of anger as a part of her tirade against Americans; she could not have known what a mortal blow she was striking.

Since his first hint of Alison's fate, three days before, he had tried to reason its possibility away. He had sought reassurance in every scrap of evidence to the contrary, yet he'd felt in his heart that Alison was the woman. In time of trouble, her father's character predominated in her; like him, she would confide in any shallow device or shift that promised a prompt success; her courage became rashness and disregard of consequences; her strength of will became willfullness. Despite his pleas and warning at Boston, she had accepted Stanhope Damer's promise of marriage because it appeared the readiest and easiest way of escaping the poverty she dreaded. It followed then that she would go desperately from expedient to expedient as her condition worsened. There was a terrible logic in what had befallen her. He felt like one who had witnessed the performance of a tragic drama, aware from the start that a catastrophe must end it, yet ignorant of the action and powerless to affect its course. Now the curtain had descended and the footlights were put out. Only pity and anger remained—pity for her tragic fault, anger at the world's ways and for a noble thing corrupted. Please God, he would never see her again.

Spent and saddened but at last calm, he paused before a house in Smith Street, drawn by the cheerful light that shone from its small-pained windows. It was the Three Pigeons tavern, a small place of resort much in favor with the gentlemen of the army, and it promised company. What kind, he cared not, for any company would be preferable to his own. The thought of his cheerless attic room appalled him no less than the loneliness of the streets.

When he entered, he found the long table occupied by a club of about a dozen officers over which Blythe was presiding. He bowed to Blythe who greeted him boisterously, and also to Major Robert Donkin who was present. The tapster served him with a glass of brandy at the counter and he drank it standing. The officers were in high fettle, toasting one another and singing songs. Although he was not of their fellowship, he was something cheered by their mirth.

"You, there! You Prentiss—" Major Donkin called to him. "Have you sent back the proofs of my book to the press? Confound you, if you have, for there's a note I

must add on page 190. You'll not believe this, gentlemen," he announced to the others, "but I had a perfect
inspiration this morning whilst I was shaving. There I
stood, staring at my face in the glass, when it came to
me."

"That you were a damned unhandsome fellow?"

"Nay, Blythe, not at all. 'Twas a new thought for the
chapter I've writ on measures to balk the rebels, and a
notable stroke 'twill be if it's attempted. What would
most affright those bloody-minded dogs, thought I? And
then, of a sudden, I had it. Smallpox. Nothing affrights
the provincials like smallpox. So why should we not dip
Indian arrows in the matter of the disease and have
them twanged off by our skirmishers?"

Some three or four of the company applauded with
boozy enthusiasm but the rest sat silent like birds in a
thunder gust and looked one to another with expres-
sions of surprise and distaste.

"You're jesting, of course," said Blythe.

"I was never more serious in my life."

"I should blush to confess it then."

"And why, sir?" demanded Donkin, starting up and
oversetting his glass in his vehemence.

"Because what you propose is inhuman, and unworthy of a British officer."

"Is it any more inhuman," Donkin shouted, "than
their sniping at our sentries and hanging our foragers—or their riflemen taking aim at an officer's gor-
get?"

"I don't set up as censor of enemy morals."

"Yet you dare to censor mine. Pray remember, sir,
that I'm your superior in rank."

"Oh, if you take that tack," answered Blythe with a

sneer, "we'll talk no more. Gentlemen, so far as I'm concerned, this club stands adjourned." He rose to his feet and walked, a little unsteadily, towards the door. The landlord bustled up with his hat and cloak.

"You'll hear more of this," Donkin called out. "Damme, if you don't."

"You know where I lodge," Blythe answered indifferently. And then to John: "Come along, my dear Prentiss. I've a bottle or two at my quarters that we can discuss. And we'll talk of high and noble things 'til we've quite forgot this fellow and his schemes."

"You've seen how civil war can debauch a man," he continued as he walked with John up Queen Street. "Yon Donkin was a decent fellow to begin with, but a year's campaigning here has made him a fool—and a vicious fool as it seems."

After he had rummaged out the promised bottles at his quarters, Blythe was soon tipsy again and John ventured to reprove him for it.

"Aye, you're altogether right," Blythe answered, nodding his head with drunken gravity. "A man should never quench his wits. But I've ample reason to tipple tonight. We've had bad news. I can say naught of it, save that I shan't have time to finish my play about Cromwell and the whole promising venture at the theater will be dished. A pity it is, after all our labors—for those who'll be left here are certain to botch what they do." He seated himself carefully in an easy chair and looked up owlishly at John. "By the look of you, you've had bad news too. Did the Forbes deny you?"

Fuddled as he was, he saw at once that he had touched the wrong string. By way of putting John at ease, he began to babble at random and he settled at last on the subject of British headquarters. All was at odds there, he said, over information that was reaching the rebels. Sir William was determined to ferret out the sources of their intelligence. Too many foraging parties had been ambushed in Jersey by American regulars and militia who appeared to know exactly where they should lie in wait for their prey.

" 'Tis all absurd, you know," Blythe said, sitting with his legs asprawl, his tongue thick. "Fetch me a glass, if you please. Ah, thank you. The true Falernian. As I say, 'tis all absurd. No one at headquarters has blabbed; to that I'll make oath. The truth is that the foragers scant their outpost work and come to grief through their own fault. My dear Prentiss, your glass is empty. 'Tis a reproach to me. Fill it at once, or I'm your enemy."

"If I were truly your friend," replied John, "I'd thrust the cork in the bottle and bundle you off to bed."

"Would you rob me of my one solace? My one means of escape from the contemplation of fallen human nature? Prentiss, my friend—my innocent provincial—my learned but artless schoolmaster—'tis clear the higher forms of depravity are unknown to you, else you'd be tipsy too for grief that such things be. I'm not so fortunate, and something has chanced today that's left even me shaken. I'll tell it you, for your instruction—but in confidence, mind you! In strictest confidence, lest my neck pay for it. Come spring, I must take the field with my regiment."

"That may be irksome," said John, smiling, "but it's hardly a form of depravity."

"Ah, but wait! I've only spoken the prologue. The

drama's still to come, and also the moral. You'll remember that we attempted a march into New York from Canada last year—Carleton led it, but he came to a stand at the lakes and nothing resulted. This year, the scheme's been revived but with a difference. Suppose the troops here in the city were to reduce the rebel forts in the Hudson Highlands and make a junction with the invaders from Canada—at Albany, say. What then? We'd have the rebel northern army trapped. What's more, we'd have cut the New England colonies off from their southern brethren. And as in my estimation of this war the Yankees are its head, as the Virginians are its heart, we could end the trouble with a single, killing blow. Do you follow me, Prentiss?"

"I believe so," said John, striving hard to keep the excitement he felt from showing in his face. "It seems a worthy plan."

"A masterpiece. Men have won dukedoms for less. Now hark ye to what's happened, and judge if I fuddle myself without reason. 'Twas decided that Burgoyne would command the march out of Canada this spring. He'd made interest in London with the Ministry and they approved of him and the plan. A good fellow is John Burgoyne, and a fair playwright too; I knew him at home—but that's no matter." He paused, shaking his head as if to clear it. Then he hurried on in a rush of words, now clearly spoken and passionate, now mumbling and slurred. "We come now to human depravity, and to a certain great man. What doth Sir William Howe about all this? Does he offer his fullest aid to his brother-in-arms? Does he sink his own ambitions in the nation's interest? Not he. He writes to Germain at the

Colonial Office—he gave me the letter to copy this
morning—and he says that he'll move the bulk of the
army south. Philadelphia is the mainspring of the rebellion, says he, and it must be taken immediately. 'Tis a
lie of course. He goes south because he's jealous of
Burgoyne and hopes to hobble him. To be sure, he
promises Germain that he'll come north after his conquest in time to support the invasion—but that's a lie
too. The stupidest ranker knows that he cannot do it.
It's a tale of a cock and a bull, fit to bemuse only a dull
fool like Germain who's three thousand miles away. But
as Germain is the only man he need convince, the
thing's as good as done. And now, sir, have I proved my
point? Here's an army risked and a victory skimped.
Here's King and country be damned—and all for vanity,
all for envy! Heard you ever so moral a tale as this? And
what but good wine can wash it down."

"A shocking tale it is indeed," said John with all caution. "I shall be sorry to lose your company, Captain.
And when will that be? Have you heard when you'll
march?"

"Mustn't tell you that—never discuss orders." All his
animation had left Blythe; he slumped in his chair,
looking pettish and sullen, his eyes half-closed. "Dirty
work to do and dirty men to do it," he muttered. And
then in a louder tone: "The bottle. Pass me the bottle,
man—and spare me your good advice."

Very soon after, the glass fell from his hand, his head
rolled to one side and he was asleep.

John took a blanket from the bed and wrapped it
around the sleeping man who stirred restlessly but did
not wake. For a long moment, he stood looking down at

Blythe's flushed face; then he raked ashes over the fire and snuffed the candles. He had no scruple over what he must do.

A patrol stopped him near the corner of King Street but the soldiers made no difficulties after seeing his pass. What would they have done, he thought, had they known what news he was carrying in his head? Enthused and excited, he fairly ran to Hanover Square, never considering the lateness of the hour until he was at the tailor's doorstep. No light showed in the house. No servants slept there, as he knew. And if he beat on the door to arouse Higgins, the noise would attract a dangerous notice by the neighbors. It were prudent that he wait until morning, yet he prayed that he would not betray himself before then. The answer to the great question was his in trust but the good of his country required that he reveal it. He must betray the confidence of one man that thousands of men might profit. He felt as if the secret were written all over his face.

Gaine himself answered John's knock at his own door, making a vast bother over undoing the bolts and chains.

"Ungodly hours ye keep," grumbled the master. "You could sleep in the street this night, only I was sitting up over my ledger. With Blythe again, were ye? A sorry day it was when first you took up with that wastrel. Friend Higgins was here, looking for you. You must call on him in the morning. He has some task for you, and I've given him my consent."

CHAPTER TWELVE

JOHN WAS early at the tailor's house next morning but he found Higgins already with his workmen, engaged in cutting out a coat.

"I've some scrivener's work for you," he greeted John, "—writing out bills and the like. Go you up to my sitting-room where it's quiet. I'll come to you presently with my books of account."

John paced restlessly about the well-remembered room for a quarter of an hour. When the tailor appeared at last, John gave him no chance to speak but poured out his story almost in a breath.

"The finger of God is in it!" exclaimed Higgins when John had done. "And to think that I summoned you here to bid you lie close for a time! The enemy's scented something amiss at his headquarters and all Americans are suspect—those in especial who crack bottles with staff officers. What's worse," he went on, looking dismayed, "they've broken my links with our army. Three of our trusted couriers are taken in Westchester and hanged. How shall we get your news to the General's ear?"

"As you've never made me privy to your secrets," John replied, "I've nothing to suggest."

" 'Tis of no consequence now," said Higgins impatiently. "If you must know, we made use of the traffic of trade between here and the neutral ground. Men rode in from the army to Tarrytown or Eastchester, posing as cattle drovers. Thither to meet them went William Mooney's runners—peddlers, Negro men, lads disguised in women's clothes. They brought out intelligence sometimes by word of mouth, but oftener 'twas hid in chapbooks and pious tracts—all printed by Master Hugh Gaine, no less. We noted significant words in the books with a pin-prick, either under or over; the runners delivered them at the north; and General Washington had our news as fast as express riders could carry the books to Captain Hamilton for decipherment. We'd arranged for a like system to Morristown, but Van Buskirk's Greencoats are swarming in Jersey now, to say naught of British forage parties—and all's at a stand 'til our people hit on some sure means of eluding them."

"And when will that be?"

"Who knows?" Higgins shook his head. "A week, perhaps."

"Why shouldn't I carry the news? I must go to the army at any event."

"Not as yet, my dear man. They'd take you in Jersey before you'd journeyed a mile. You must have a guide who knows the byroads."

"Then find me one. Even a day's delay might cost us the advantage. The General must have time to warn the northern forces; he must make his own plan to thwart the British march south. And even if the British were

still drowsing, you daren't trust a mere runner with
what I have to tell. If your fellow had wit, he might be
tempted to sell the information back to Howe. If he
lacked wit, he'd never be believed at Morristown.
Whereas I'm the discoverer of this scheme and can stand
questioning about it. I must go, I tell you, and at once."

"All that you say is true," answered Higgins. "And
yet—"

"For another thing," John pressed on, "there's one
arrived lately in the city who knows me well and might
betray me. The sooner I'm off and away, the better for
you and for all of us."

"Go back to the shop," said Higgins, with the air of a
man who had made up his mind. "I'll send for you later
when I've found a way. Meanwhile, be as discreet as you
can. Your master's a shrewd, suspicious body and you've
much too lofty a manner for your station. I wonder he
hasn't found you out before this."

An angry Hugh Gaine met John as he entered the
bookshop.

"I trust that your lordship feels able to work after last
night's frisk," he began with heavy sarcasm. "There's
plenty for you to do, and I counsel you to set about it at
once. I've no place here for roisterers and lallygaggers.
I'm off to the Exchange," he concluded, taking up his
cloak and hat. "See that I find all in order when I return."

John labored undisturbed for almost an hour. He was
grateful for the lack of custom and for the quiet, broken
only by the comfortable noise of the pressmen at work
beyond the double door. His mind was fevered with the

thought of leaving the city and with a nervous anxiety lest something untoward occur to destroy his hopes. Let Higgins only prove resourceful and this tedious masquerade would soon be over; he would be himself again, devoting himself once more to useful pursuits. After long thought he had reconciled himself to the idea of an intervention by the French, although he did not relish the notion and was far from sharing the tailor's confidence, and Doctor Franklin's, in the honor and promises of King Louis' ministers. However, that would be a matter to be settled all in good time, like the reckoning that must be cast up with the native politicians and Congress.

Dusting and ordering the books and other articles displayed on the tables, he had worked his way almost to the back of the shop when he heard the street door open. Looking round, he saw that a smart chariot had drawn up outside; a soldier-footman was handing in a lady and her maidservant. The lady paused an instant at the doorway, outlined against the gray morning light and her face in shadow, but he knew her; he knew her every feature even before she threw back the hood of her fur-trimmed capuchin cloak and stepped forward.

His breath caught in his throat. From the first rumor of Alison Cunningham's presence in the city, he had known in his heart that this meeting with her must take place. It was a thing fated, as the ancients believed. He had feared it and expected it but he had not planned for it, and he felt rise in him that self-same senseless anticipation of failure that had ever possessed him when he was confronted with a situation beyond reason, beyond his own control.

"What a horrid clutter!" she exclaimed in a pettish and humorsome tone after the merest glance over the foremost table. "Here's everything and nothing. You, fellow—" she called to John. "Do you wait here? Come, pray, and find me a copy of the *Sentimental Journey*. 'Tis writ by Mr. Sterne."

She would recognize him, she would cry out in alarm, and he would be taken. To hope otherwise were folly.

Since there was no help for it, he walked slowly toward her but she did not look attentively at him until he stood beside her. Her eyes widened then and her mouth drew tight but she gave no other sign of recognition. How little she had changed, he thought! He had expected some radical alteration in her look and manner, foolishly enough, but here she stood in the dim light of the shop, slim, boyish even, her head held proudly as of old.

"Simpson, my dear," she said, turning to the lumpish maidservant who waited at a little remove from her, "take this sample of silk to the mercer's next door and match it. 'Twill save time, and your eyes are sharper than mine. I'll have nine yards of it, and five of the like quality in green if he has it. Fly now, and stay for me at the carriage."

And when the woman had gone:

"You looked better in your own hair, John," she said. "I marvel to find you in a wig." She smiled as she spoke but her deep blue eyes did not smile. He could not trust himself to say a word.

"I shan't ask what you're doing here," she went on. "I'm sure you've a reason for what you do—you always had, be it good or ill. You need fear nothing from me,

John. And now, if you'll be so kind, fetch me Mr. Sterne's book."

The book was close to his hand and he took it up. He dared not look her in the face and he found himself studying the binding of the two small volumes with an almost painful absorption.

"I've thought of you many times," he said. "I've wished it were otherwise with us."

"If wishes were horses, beggars would ride," she replied with an air of indifference. "I never think on the past, nor should you. You made your choice at Wendham when you broke your word to me."

"I gave you my reasons for that in Boston. You could have waited for me there."

"Aye, if I'd been so minded. I remember how eloquent you were that evening. 'Twas so unlike you, and you almost persuaded me."

"You had a better alternative, to be sure."

"I did what seemed best to me," she answered, in a sharper tone but with no other recognition of his irony. "At the least, my father's provided for. He's an inspector of the King's stores at Halifax."

"And you?"

"I'm quite content." He thought of Blythe's mother suddenly, and wondered if all women were so supple and artful.

"Tell me about yourself," she continued, kindly enough but with an air of patronage, as he thought. "I must judge from your looks and your situation here that you've fared badly, and I'm sorry for it. Or are you playing at spy again? 'Tis a bad business at best, and a worse one to attempt for a failing cause."

"Have you had any word of Richard?" he asked, ignoring her question. No matter how she galled him, he would not shame her with his knowledge of her condition.

"Only what I told you at Boston. All loyal folk are slighted in London, they say. Better your brother had stayed in America."

And snatched at opportunity, he thought—and sold himself, even as you have?

"I'm properly circumstanced now," she said, with a complacency that stirred his anger. "I've all I could wish for. And when I go to London—"

"As the Honorable Mrs. Damer?"

She mantled at that, the blood coloring her cheek and brow.

"Nay, that's all by," she answered, looking at him with an expression he could not fathom. "We parted unfriends at Halifax and he's returned to England."

"I'm grieved to hear it."

"You needn't be." She shrugged contemptuously. "I'm truly glad of it. A monstrous jealous, heedless man he was, though free enough with his money when I needed help. Come the war's end, when we get our property back, I'll look about me for a worthy settlement. I shall marry an Englishman, I think."

"And wear your diamonds to Ranelagh?" he asked, bitterly echoing her brag to him at Boston. Her grand airs and her assumption that she could gull him thus easily had shaken his resolution to spare her. "And go to Court perhaps?"

"Why should I not go to Court?"

"You can answer that better than I."

She stared at him, her hand going unconsciously to her heart. Her face was like snow but her eyes burned with a sad light.

"So you know, then," she said at length, and the pretense and arrogance of her previous speeches seemed pitiful now like a small child's evasions. He was seized with sorrow for her and disgust of himself. "Why should you censure me? The blame is yours as much as mine."

"I to blame?"

"You, you, you," she broke out with sudden vehemence, her mouth trembling. "Your reason and your conscience have ruined us both. All's gone wrong since you failed me at Wendham." She paused and struggled to master herself; then she said with a gentleness and dignity that cut him like a scourge: "We took each his own road, John. The time's gone by for regrets. I should not have railed at you. We've lived an age in these two years. We're no longer the people we were."

He felt that he should take her in his arms and comfort her with kindness and promises, but he could not. She had spoken only the truth. She was alike in physical semblance to the girl whose imagined presence had for so long delighted and tormented him, yet in all else she had subtly changed.

"I learned this much from Damer," she continued, "—to keep myself free of attachments and to enjoy what I can. I live from day to day and it satisfies me."

"You're satisfied to be Howe's mistress? To be the talk and nayword of the city?"

"Have you any better prospect to show me?" He was silent.

"The world's turned upside down," she said, her

voice confident once again, her face a mask. "I cannot set it right—no more can you. What could you offer me now? The love of a hunted man with naught to expect but a prison or the gallows?"

"Ah, there you're wrong," he answered, his heart quickening with new hope. "If that's your sole concern, dismiss it. The victory will be ours in time. You need only be patient and trust me."

"All else changes but you, John. You've still the same fantasy, still the same stubborn faith and self-deceit. As well I know, 'tis your nature to be dogged and proud— but I'm not so. I cannot dream of what's to be; I must accept what is."

"At the cost of honor?"

"At any cost, so long as I survive."

"For how long?" he demanded. "For a month? A year, perhaps? And then what? Who's a friend to a cast mistress? Alison, for the love of God, consider!"

"Do you think that I haven't? Do you think so lowly of me?"

"I love you," he said simply.

"In spite of all that's chanced?" She smiled and shook her head.

"I shall always love you, no matter how high you soar or how low you sink."

"Will you give me a proof of it?" she cried with a change of mood that quite confounded him. "Will you swear the oaths and take His Majesty's pardon? 'Tis not too late. Come with me to Sir William—now! He's not the monster you may think him. He'll fume and frown and call me cheat, but he'll laugh at last and let us both go free. We'll be wed, John, as we thought to be once.

Aye, and we'll home to Wendham if it please you. I swore to you that I'd never return to that place but I'm wiser grown in these last weary months. I'll tend the garden and turn the spit and spin, and you'll go jog-trot round the town to your sick. Peace or war, rich or poor, 'twill make no matter to us. And we'll be the kinder for all the evil we've known."

The joyous shining of her face and the eagerness with which she spoke almost persuaded him that she could be his again, half lovely woman and half wilful child, just as on that wild Sabbath when the townsfolk had mobbed her father's house and he had protected and won her. His spirit rose like Icarus and as swiftly fell. For the condition of his happiness was a treason, a betrayal of all honest folk, of his brothers-in-arms, of himself. He was wholly devoted to the cause of America; his oath, if he took it, would be a blasphemy. Moreover, he had given Higgins his word to go to Morristown. He had forced the decision on the tailor, and truly no other messenger would serve. Men's lives were in his hands and the hope of the young nation for victory. He was the elected instrument, and to seek his own pleasure now would be unforgivable on earth or in heaven. As on the day of Concord when he had been forced to choose between his duty and his desire, as in the dark and wintry Boston lane where he had been tempted once again to prefer his selfish ends to the common weal, so now— and in heart-breaking measure.

"You needn't speak," said Alison. "Your answer's in your face."

"I'd give my life for you," he burst out, "but I cannot do what you ask."

"It seems a small thing beside your life," she replied

with deep bitterness. "Yet I might have guessed you'd deny me. You talk of love but what do you know of it? 'Tis your own stubborn will that you love and cherish; I'm nothing to you in comparison. Conscience, you call it! Duty!" Her laugh was sudden and harsh. "I wish you joy of it. Look to it for consolation when you think to what you've condemned me."

At the door, she turned and spoke again:

"Your secret's safe with me. There's been enough of meanness and betrayal."

For the moment, he seemed rooted where he stood, speechless and incapable of action. But as he watched the footman assist her into the chariot and her maid-servant climb in beside her, he ran out into the street, still clutching the books in his hand. He knew not what he should say, but it was no matter. The chariot was already in motion and she did not so much as glance back at him.

She was gone, and her passing had closed the book of youth with a dark and terrible page. Of all his ideal conceptions, none was left to him but the vision of his country's triumph and the part he must play in it. The chariot, now lurching on to Queen Street, bore much of his old life away with it, corrupted with her corruption, like the stink of dead lilies in a closed room.

He went back into the shop, wondering at his own calm of mind as he put the *Sentimental Journey* back in its place on the table. It was like the numbness that tempered the first pain of a wound, he thought; later he must surely suffer.

He looked round sharply, hearing the door open. But it was only Higgins, breathless and anxious.

"You're alone?" he asked. "Can the men in the other

room hear what we say?" John answered that they could not; the noise of the press would prevent it.

"You must set off this afternoon," the tailor continued in a low voice. "You must be at Delamater's farm near Elizabethtown before midnight. 'Tis the first considerable holding to the northwest of the town on the road to Springfield. One of Jacob Arnold's Light Horse waits there in the barn on another errand, but he'll guide you to Morristown. The sign is "Vigilance", the countersign "Trenton"—mark them well, for they may mean your life. You'll be put ashore near Elizabethport by the sloop *Alida*. She sails from King's Wharf at three o'clock with supplies for the British at Amboy, but we've reasoned with her captain and he's agreed to run down the Kills and see you safe. He'd better," said Higgins grimly. "We've kinfolk of his our prisoners in Connecticut. 'Tis a rickety scheme but the best that offers and you must take the risk. You'll be dressed as a sailor. William Mooney has the slops ready for you and he'll go with you to the wharf. Be at William's house in Nassau Street by two o'clock. Meanwhiles, go on working here and invent some plausible tale to account for your leaving."

CHAPTER THIRTEEN

JOHN AND the watchful William Mooney turned off Broadway into Cortlandt Street and began to thread their way westward to the King's Wharf through a slow-moving press of market carts and army wagons. The afternoon was bleak, cloudy and cold; a mist hung low over the Hudson and veiled the river's farther shore.

Mooney's saturnine face was glum. He had declared himself doubtful of the success of the venture while John was dressing at his house, and after counseling his companion to feign drunkenness on their walk since a poor sot of a tarry breeks returning to his ship would be least suspected, he had relapsed into silence. This circumstance pleased John who was in a state of mind altogether fatalistic and high-wrought. He would not soon forget his last hour in Gaine's shop. Ambrose Serle had held him in talk until almost two o'clock and he had feared he must be late for his appointment with Mooney. And Alison's image kept returning before his mind's eye, each time bringing him a further sadness and sense of frustrated hopes. Indeed he had experienced a mite of cheer only once this day—when he had

191

flung off his wig for the last time. The action had
marked a return to his own identity, an end to chicane
and imposture. Mooney had given him a loaded pistol.
He felt it now under his coarse frieze jacket and hoped
he would not have to use it.

Only a few score yards remained to be traversed before they reached the wharf gate. Up ahead and to the
right, the carts and wagons were turning in at the entrance to the forage yard or else leaving it; on the left
was a low drinking house through whose half-open door
came the sound of men's voices raised in a sad chorus.
He recognized the tune as one the Scottish soldiers
sang—

> *Lochaber, no more,*
> *Lochaber, no more;*
> *We'll maybe return to Lochaber no more—*

That was the English of it, but the men in the drinking
house were voicing it in their own barbarous tongue.

"Say naught if we're challenged," warned Mooney
out of the corner of his mouth. "Act as fou as you can
and leave the talking to me. I don't like the look of what
I see by the wharf."

And with reason, thought John. The open ground at
the foot of the wharf was fair crawling with armed men
—not regulars, but Tory Rangers. The British were
building works of some sort and the labor was being
performed by American prisoners under heavy guard.
Just to the left of the wharf gate was the head of a long
trench which John and William Mooney had to pass
close by as they approached the guard house—so close indeed that the abject air and mechanical motions of one

of the unfortunates digging in the frozen ground drew John's attention as somehow familiar. When he was abreast of the man and no more than six feet distant, the fellow straightened up from his work, stood erect, and stared at John with a dazed and pitiful look of inquiry. Shocked and sorry, John returned the look. He knew the man although the prisoner had aged thirty years since their last meeting and his eyes had death in them—it was Shawcross, the Marylander, the malingerer at Fort Washington. Their glances remained fixed on each other for what seemed a long time but John could not tell whether Shawcross had recognized him or not.

"Let be your gawking. Play the sot as I bid you," said Mooney in an anxious, angry whisper. "Will you have us both hanged?"

Two soldiers had emerged from the guard house on observing a pair of strangers approach it—a sergeant of Rangers and a private.

"What's your business here?" demanded the sergeant brusquely and with a look of distaste at John.

"This poor drunken fellow's my business," Mooney answered the man confidently, seizing John by the arm as he affected to stagger and seemed like to fall. "He's an old servant of mine who came kindly to pay me a visit this noon. He went to sea to better himself, so he did— and will you look at him now! A pretty pass he's at! Ah, sergeant, the drink is a terrible curse altogether. It steals a man's brains away out of his own mouth. But to an-swer your question—I've kept him company here like a good Christian to see him safe aboard his ship, which is the *Alida* that I see yonder on the left side of the pier. As for me, my name is William Mooney. I'm a good friend to government and a faithful subject of King George, God bless him."

"Aye, I know you," the sergeant replied. "I was journeyman to your neighbor Jacob Oakes, before I set up for myself in the upholstery trade and was ruined by this war. You're a loyal man and well I know it—but loyal or not, Master Mooney, you must show me a pass from the main guard ere either of you set foot on the wharf. We Rangers have the duty here—and that means an end to slipshod watch-keeping."

"We haven't the time to get a pass," protested Mooney. "Be reasonable, man! The ship will have sailed before we could foot it to Wall Street and back—much less the time we must bide whilst the clerks there fumble and fuss. Will you have it on your conscience that you lost this poor man his employment? And he a family man, with children and a wife to be fed?"

"I'd oblige you, sir, if I could, but I've my orders. If your friend's undone, he must thank himself for it."

During this exchange and several thereafter in which Mooney wheedled and threatened, John teetered on his feet and regarded the sergeant with a fixed and stupid grin. Aware that Shawcross was still staring intently up at him from the head of the trench, he waited with his nerves drawn tight as a fiddle string for some word or motion that would betray him. In the weakened state of the poor prisoner's intellects, it was inevitable that his recognition of John would be followed by action of some kind. So that John was near to shouting with relief when the sergeant at last relented.

"Well enough, well enough," he said wearily. "Let him go on. If it were anybody but you, Master Mooney,

I'd say be damned to you both. This business could cost me my shoulder knot."

After a hurried word of thanks, Mooney bade John farewell (not forgetting to urge sobriety on him in future), gave him a hearty shove forward that sent him stumbling down the wharf, and betook himself off in the opposite direction as fast as he could walk.

The *Alida*'s people were hoisting her jib and she strained at her lines in a strong breeze from the northeast; a black-bearded man at her wheel was waving to John to make haste. Instinct urged John to run for it but he clung to his assumed character and continued to stumble drunkenly on. Ten or so feet remained before he could jump from the wharf to the heaving deck. And then a great tumult broke out behind him. Still moving forward, he looked back over his shoulder.

An officer had appeared at the guard house and was berating the sergeant in high tones. Almost at the same time, a cry of "Rouse! Rouse out!" was raised and soldiers came running in answer from the forage yard and from every direction.

"After that man!" the officer shouted, turning from the sergeant. "Bring him here to me!"

The soldiers were at a loss to obey. Some were of the opinion that the order applied to Mooney who was by now a good distance up Cortlandt Street; others that John was meant; but the most stood irresolute.

Their minds were soon made up for them. With a wild, wordless cry, Shawcross sprang out of the trench by the guard house and ran off northward along the beach. His seeming attempt at an escape drew the notice of the Rangers away from both Mooney and John, and although the other prisoners made no trial of flight they set up a shouting that confounded the soldiers still more. The greater part of the guard started after the lean, scarecrow figure that ran with a pathetic slowness as if the pace were long unfamiliar to him; a scatter of shots rang out; and just as John reached the *Alida* and stood ready to leap down on her deck from the string-piece, he saw the fleeing man fling his hands in the air and fall headlong on the shingle of the beach. At that instant, the black-bearded man at the wheel of the vessel, cursing like a damned soul, ordered the lines let go. John had only time to hurl himself forward and land aboard on all-fours before the *Alida* bore swiftly away.

Her two crewmen were hauling up the mainsail and she was already in the stream and heading south of west when John rose to his feet and stood unsteadily on the canted deck. Was Shawcross wounded, or dead? He would never know, in all probability, yet he owed his freedom to that poor, crackbrained creature who had sacrificed himself for one who deserved little enough of him. Here was another debt to be paid—but there was no time now to think of that, or to philosophize. The master of the *Alida* was regarding him with an unfriendly eye.

"Ye've left a proper broil back there," complained the bearded man in a grating voice. "I'll hear of it from the harbor-master, no doubt. Yon Mooney's a liar. He swore 'twould be all on the quiet."

John made him no reply. The master was a Tory by inclination and was acting under duress, so that he could not be trusted; the crewmen were stolid appearing louts who seemed to lack wit for anything but their captain's orders. They were three to his one—but the pistol under his coat was reassuring and the salt smell of the sea had wonderfully revived him. He moved over by the wheel and stood close beside the master.

"How long before we touch the Jersey shore?" he asked after about ten minutes' sailing. They had altered course and were driving down the bay as he thought, but it was impossible for him to be sure. The mist hung about the *Alida* in wind-whipped patches and was a dull gray swirling wall at no long distance before them. The master, peering anxiously ahead, only grunted in answer.

"Look sharp up there for floats of ice!" he called to the seaman in the bow, and he had barely closed his mouth when the lookout gave a loud halloo.

"A sail—dead ahead," the man shouted. And then— " 'Tis a cutter, sir."

"A man-of-war's boat," cried the captain. "Now damn me if I've any luck today! They never patrol at this hour —never 'til now. Lookee, Mister whatever your name is," he went on, turning to John. "I hadn't bargained for this. I must bring-to and be searched. And you must take your chance of it, for I'll swear that you forced me to take you aboard."

"And never a truer word would you say," replied John, drawing out the pistol and clapping it against the captain's head. "Make good your escape, or I'll blow out your brains. You there!" he called to the crewmen. "Make no false moves or I'll shoot this man where he stands."

The *Alida* sheered off to starboard like a bird wheeling in flight, whereupon the cutter ran up a signal accompanied by a loud command to heave-to that was bawled through a trumpet and sounded eerily over the water. At the same time, the cutter prepared to change course and follow. The *Alida* was making up fast and passed the cutter abeam a little more than a musket shot's distance; the following wind held, rolling up the mist before it into a solid cover to southwestward and bringing with it yet another providence—a squall of freezing rain and snow.

The *Alida* flew on the new course, heeling well over and dousing her decks with salt spray. The cutter, at last in chase, let off a heavy fire of small arms blind in the mist and continued to do so for some time. Happily, none of the shot took effect.

At length the firing, after diminishing in volume, ceased. The master, who had been standing like a statue at the wheel, broke silence.

"They've abandoned the chase," he said, an odd note of satisfaction in his voice. "We've given them leg bail. Ah, but she's a sweetheart, my *Alida!* And now, sir, will you take your damned pistol from my head? You're in no danger now."

"So you say."

"Aye, and you can believe it. We're off the entrance to the Kill and no King's ship will follow us in this weather."

"How do you know where we are?"

"By my nose," the master replied contemptuously. "I can smell the shore here, night or day, foggy or fair. I was raised in this place."

The wind lessened in force after they rounded Constable's Point and the tide was adverse, so that it was a weary time of haul up and haul down, tack and trim, before the master brought the *Alida* to and ordered one of his men to row John ashore in the boat.

"I'll venture my ship no closer in this murk," he said. "We'll land you near the new ferry. A little way in from the landing, you'll come on a dry path through the meadows. Follow it to a highroad and thence into the town. 'Tis a good three miles and a bit. Nay, thank me not," he concluded sullenly. "I want no Whiggish thanks. I'll be content if Mooney keeps his word and my kinfolk come to no harm."

The crewman rowed John to the shore in total silence, backing his oars and withdrawing before John had splashed through the crusts of ice in the shallows to what appeared to be a marshy beach.

After several casts about in the snowy gloom, he found the path; it was a mere cartway that wound through overgrown and frozen swamps and was hardly to be distinguished from them. Soon the path was closely bordered by dense growths of cedar, drooping beneath their burdens of ice and snow. It was easier to follow now, yet John found himself becoming more apprehensive as he slipped and stumbled along. What should he do if Elizabethtown were held by Tory raiders? And how was he to find Delamater's farm without asking questions which might excite suspicion? "Northwest of the town—!" The phrase had sounded satisfactory enough in the comparative safety of New York but it was almost without meaning in this wintry wilderness. Stubbornly, he fought down all thoughts but one—he was free, and his continued freedom depended on his own resolution and courage. Wet, cold, and conscious now of a vast fatigue, he pressed on as quickly as he could.

When he had journeyed about a mile, so far as he could reckon, the wind soughing mournfully in the trees and whirling the snow in gusts about him, he paused for a little and considered what he should do. There was still no sign of the highroad; yet if he left the path and struck off through the woods he might flounder hours away and be in worse case at the end. The path was interminable but it must lead somewhere. Taking some comfort from the thought that no way-farers would be abroad in such a night, he struck off again and, on rounding a twist in the path, found himself quite unexpectedly at its junction with a broad highway. Hard by the end of the path was a lonely, deserted building of two stories; a toppled inn sign lay broken on the snow before it.

Assuming that the directions given him were correct, he should turn left on the road and walk about two miles to reach Elizabethtown. The prospect revived him and he increased his pace, considering at the same time what story he might tell to account for himself should he be challenged in the town. None seemed worthy of credit; certainly, he thought, he would have believed none of them if he were the questioner.

Within a half-mile, the road displayed signs of habitation in the neighborhood; hedges ran beside it and the remains of wooden fences plundered for firewood. The snow had ceased to fall and the bitter wind had subsided. However, it was full dark, and when John saw what he took to be a flash of lantern-light at no great distance before him, he was curiously heartened. Friend, or enemy? He could not tell. Yet he must speak to someone sooner or later and be put to the test. Why not now?

He found no one at the place where he had seen the light. The road curved slightly to the right there, with trees thick on one side, and on the other what appeared to be a wagon-track winding off to some distant farmstead. He stood and rested a moment, swallowing his disappointment and rousing himself for further effort— and then without sound or warning he was seized on from behind, his arms were pinioned, and he was dragged into the cover of the woods.

A lantern was shone on his face, dazzling his eyes.

" 'Taint nobody from this part," a voice said. "Them's sailor clothes he has on. P'raps he's a deserter."

John could make out now that he was the prisoner of some ten or twelve irregulars, all with weapons at the ready, save for the two who continued to hold him fast.

"Wag yer tongue, Jack," commanded the speaker—a squat, strongly built man who was apparently the leader of the band. "What's yer business here?"

It was impossible to tell from their look which side his captors favored. They might be Tories; they might be Jersey militiamen; or they might well be marauders devoted to either side as convenience dictated. There were many of such a kidney who cloaked knavery with an assumed patriotism or loyalty, raiding isolated farms and settlements and retreating thereafter to outlaw strongholds in the hills. Whichever they might be, John knew that he stood in mortal peril.

"I'm a seaman from Massachusetts who's come ashore," he answered. "I'm looking for work."

"What town're ye from?" demanded the leader after a pause and a further close scrutiny.

"Salem."

"He's a liar," spoke up another of the band. "He talks like a colleger—or an Englishman."

"Well, what think ye?" asked the leader, turning to his men.

"I think we'd best look alive if we mean to visit Tory Benson tonight," said a gray-bearded fellow, hefting his fowling-piece and staring hard at John. "Hang him. That'll teach his like what the Jarsey militia will do."

"Wait!" cried John, snatching at a straw. "If you're of the right side, I'll tell you the truth. I'm a courier from New York—an American like yourselves—and I must be at Delamater's barn before midnight. If you're of this region, you'll know the place; I was told it was northwest of the town." The militiamen looked one to another. "I'm to meet a man there—a horseman from the Morristown camp," John hurried on. "He'll vouch for me."

"Nay, nay," protested the graybeard. "Hang him and have done with him. We've wasted time enough on a spy."

Fortunately for John, the rest of the militiamen were not of the same opinion.

"That farm's not a mile off by the wood paths," said one. "I votes we carry him there. He could be a true man, as he says." And a general murmur approved the proposal.

"Bind up his arms then," ordered the leader. "Stab him if he tries to run for it. If ye've lied to us, ye'll swing," he told John. "Now march!"

The militiamen set off at a trot in Indian-file, through the trees for most of the way, and then across frozen bog-land and a brook to the edge of a considerable tract of cultivated fields.

"That there's the Delamater place," said the leader, "and yonder's the barn. You Vaughan—and you Parker! Creep up on it easy. See if it's maybe a trap."

The two men went off. As no alarm was given, the remainder of the band followed after and entered the barn.

"All's well here," said the voice of Vaughan in the darkness. " 'Tis William Barber who waits. He's cousin to Francis the schoolmaster, and a cornet of Jacob Arnold's troop."

The lantern was lighted and John was thrust forward under the eye of a young man in shabby regimentals.

"Do ye know aught of this fellow?" the militia leader demanded.

"The sign is 'Vigilance,' " John burst out before the trooper could answer. "Oliver Higgins sent me. My name's John Frayne and you must guide me to the camp. John Morgan will know me there, and Baylor, and a half dozen more of the General's staff."

"He's not the man I looked to meet," said the trooper, "but he has the sign, and all the names right enough. Will you tell me your errand, Master Frayne?"

" 'Tis for the General's ear alone."

"He'll bubble it to you desperate quick with a rope around his neck," the leader growled. "Shall we make trial of it?"

"Nay, hold a little!" The young officer looked appraisingly at John. "If he were false, he'd not have refused me. He'd have had some likely yarn to spin. I'm minded to trust him. How got you clear of the city without a British pass?"

"William Mooney contrived it."

" 'Tis a sufficient answer," said the cornet to the others. "Either he's of the right side, or all our secrets are known at Howe's headquarters. Leave him with me. And a good night's hunting to you."

And when the militiamen had gone silently off:

"You'd best sleep," he told John. "Shake down a bed of hay for yourself. I must stay and watch 'til midnight but there's no need for you to keep awake."

"I was taken at Fort Washington," John began, for it seemed to him in the great relief and exultation which he was experiencing that no confidence should be withheld from the man who had saved him. "I was surgeon to the hospital—"

"Nay, now—" interrupted the cornet, kindly but firmly, "—tell me no more while you're so weary given. There'll be time enough for such talk on our ride to camp. Cheer up, man! Once we're over the Short Hills, we'll be in our own country where never an English soldier will set his foot."

CHAPTER FOURTEEN

HE STOOD in a street of a city which resembled New York and yet was not that place. It was near dusk. All about him, a great throng passed and re-passed, hurrying up and down with sad and intent faces, the faces of strangers. They paid him no heed in their restless progress; indeed he was sensible of their differ-ence from him, as if he were a spirit or they were. Of a sudden, afar off, he saw Blythe striding moodily along and he called to him, but Blythe did not answer. Then, and how it came about he knew not, he was in Mrs. Forbes's drawing-room and Alison was with him; her face was stained with tears. He found nothing he could say to her, nor did she speak. And as he strove to reach out his arms to her she receded and was gone and he was standing in the street again amid the troubled multi-tude. But now their faces were twisted with anger and they beset him on all sides, lurching against him and pummeling him without mercy.

He started awake in a cold sweat to find a man bend-ing down over him and shaking him gently. It was Colo-nel Fitzgerald, one of General Washington's aides-de-camp, and now John remembered. This was Fitzgerald's room with the sunlight streaming in at the windows; he had been brought here on his arrival at Morristown the night before.

"Up, man! Up! Turn out!" the broad-shouldered Irishman was saying. " 'Tis close on ten o'clock. The General waits for you."

When he had ridden into Morristown with Cornet Barber, John had demanded an immediate interview with General Washington, but the guards at the Arnold Tavern where the General lodged had let him know that he must wait for a seemlier time than four in the morning. Happily, George Baylor had not left head-quarters as yet to begin his new duties as a recruiter of cavalry, for Scammell, Webb, and the rest of the staff whom John had known at Boston and afterwards, had resigned to take field commands. Had not Baylor vouched for him and Fitzgerald befriended him, he would have spent the night in the guard house.

He rose, broke the thin skin of ice on the water in the wash-basin, and scrubbed his face and hands. He was still much agitated and vaporish for want of rest, and his frieze jacket and sailor's slops were hardly proper dress for a call on the commanding general, but there was no help for it.

"You'll find His Excellency a mite irritable, I fear," said Fitzgerald as they left the house and started across the snow-covered common. It was a brilliant winter's day, the sun glinting on the snow and on the icicles that hung from eave and window-sill. "Until Congress appoints more aides for him, he has only Tilghman, Johnston and me to do his work. And God knows how much he has to perplex him, poor man—more, I dare swear, than any soldier's had since the Creation."

The village of Morristown, as John now observed it by daylight, was a small place; the principal structures about the common were two churches, a building which might have been a courthouse, a recently erected powder magazine, and the two-storied tavern towards which they were making their way. A few wagons loaded with forage and fodder were moving in along the road from the west and soldiers in a wide variety of dress were everywhere. Near the southeast corner of the common, a battalion of Continentals, virtually in rags, were at drill.

"The General was wise when he chose to quarter us here," Fitzgerald remarked. "As you see, we lie in a valley screened by mountains. We can sally forth as the spirit moves us but Howe and his men would be hard put to force an entrance along the roads. Moreover, we can levy supplies off the farmers in the neighborhood the while we deny their trading with the British. Sir William's army is altogether dependent on horses for mobility. If he can't get oats and hay and corn, he's stuck as fast as a hog in a wallow, so we keep up a constant harassment of his foragers. The Jersey militia excel in ambuscades—'tis meat and drink to them."

Fitzgerald took the salute of the guardsmen who were walking sentry outside the tavern and announced that he and John were commanded to see the General. Entering a hall which ran from front to back of the building, they paused before the door of the front chamber on the south side. The aide knocked and a voice bade them enter.

George Washington was seated before a trestle table on which a great number of papers were piled in neat order. A pleasant-faced man who was assisting the General put down his pen as John and Fitzgerald came into the room, rose, and introduced himself as Colonel Tilghman, recalling very politely that he had had the pleasure of John's acquaintance just after the battle on Long Island. It was plain to John that he was expected, and he thought to himself with some little gratification that his news would soon justify his welcome. He bowed to the General who rose and bowed stiffly in answer.

"Permit me to congratulate you, sir, on your fortunate escape from the enemy," he said. "Colonel Baylor has apprised me of it. As I understand that you bring intelligence of particular moment, I have asked General Greene to come and hear it with me. We shall wait for him to join us."

In the brief interval before Greene's arrival, John studied the commander-in-chief with the closest attention. Washington had altered somewhat in appearance since John had last seen him. His tall figure was robust as ever and indicative of great reserves of strength; his manner was serene and his speech measured; but his face was gaunt and taut and his blue eyes anxious, as if the weight of care and the constant exercise of self-control were wearing on his spirit. After greeting John, he had returned to the interrupted scrutiny of his papers with complete composure. Surely, John thought with a sudden access of loyal sympathy, no one better resembled the leader of a great cause than did this grave Virginian. Please God, he was the man he seemed.

General Greene entered the room alone, exchanged

formal greetings with Washington, and took a seat at the table with the vexed and absent air of one who believed he might be more profitably employed. There had been talk among the prisoners at New York that Greene had been responsible for the decision to hold Fort Washington, and this John now remembered; it lent support to the antipathy which Greene's manner had instantly engendered in him.

"Pray begin, Mr. Frayne," said Washington.

John told his tale without interruption, citing a number of circumstances which he supposed would give it credence; at the same time he noted with growing dismay that the faces of his hearers showed forth no particular interest, much less enthusiasm.

"And so, gentlemen," he concluded, "we have it on the authority of one of Sir William Howe's own aides that the first object of the British arms this spring will be Philadelphia."

"We are grateful to you for your information," said Washington after a little pause, "and for the zeal which has brought you back to the army with it. As I recall, you were with the general hospital at Cambridge and were among those taken at Fort Washington. I believe we met last at Fort Lee. What think you of this business, General Greene?"

"A most interesting narrative. To be sure, the other intelligence which we have from New York runs counter to it, as Your Excellency is well aware. You have this only on the word of your Captain Blythe?" Greene asked, turning to John. "You did not see the letter you mention, or a copy of it?"

"No, sir."

"By your own statement," pursued Greene, "your informant was a drunkard and a wastrel—dissatisfied moreover with his country's situation and disloyal in speech of his commanding officer."

"That is true, sir. But I should suppose—"

"There's yet another aspect to consider. Have you thought, Mr. Frayne, that you might have been discovered by this man and used by him and his superiors to deceive us? Might not the whole of his friendship and confidence in you have been an elaborate device whereby a false impression of the enemy's intentions might be given us?"

"No, sir," replied John, growing angry and striving to repress it. "I should have been a fool to be so gulled."

"You'd not be the first man ever fooled, nor the last," said Greene sharply. "All of us are fallible. And there's yet a third possibility, which I mention with all reserve —that you've changed your sentiments; that you took the oaths in New York and turned your coat; that you came here deliberately with this story as a spy in British pay."

The notion was so monstrous that John could do nothing at first but stare at his inquisitor.

"I can only say, sir," he answered at long last and with a forced calm, "that I'm innocent of what you charge. Baylor and Scammell will vouch for my honesty—Gibbs too, and Doctor John Morgan of the hospital—"

"I charge you with nothing," said Greene. "We can easily establish your good faith through Higgins and Mooney in the city, and we shall do so. But you must see that your news—which is hearsay at best—can hardly persuade us."

"I fear that is true," put in Washington, shaking his head. "As for me, I cannot believe that Sir William would abandon Burgoyne, no matter what his personal animus may be. I should not wish you to think that we disregard your services," he continued to John. "That you have placed yourself in our hands is a fair proof of your truthfulness and loyalty. We are thankful to you, whatever the outcome, and I should be pleased if you put your account in writing and delivered it to me. Is there any way in which I can serve you?"

"Am I to consider myself under arrest," John asked, "until General Greene has established my good faith?"

"Nay, sir, you are free to do as you please."

"I should wish then to rejoin the medical department at the first opportunity."

"It will be a pleasure to gratify you," said Washington, his face relaxing a little from its extreme gravity. "Colonel Fitzgerald, see to what's necessary. And now, Colonel Tilghman, to our labors once again. Pray wait a little, General Greene. I must have your advice on this matter of bounty money—"

Before John and Fitzgerald had left the room, Washington was intent upon his work.

And what a piddling work it was, John thought in bitter disgust. A shuffling of papers, the while a great cause was failing! Icily courteous, deferential to Greene, devoted to petty detail, unaware of opportunity even when it was thrust on him—no wonder this martinet had gone from defeat to defeat! His measured speech, his calmness and deliberation, what were they but signs of his slowness of mind and coldness of heart?

"You'd best report to Doctor Burnet at the hospital,"

said Fitzgerald. "Tell him I'll have your papers prepared by this evening. He'll be happy to see you, I'll
wager, for he and three worthless mates have had all the
duty since young Doctor Bond fell sick. Don't be
angry," he went on as if he read John's thoughts.
"You've no notion at all what the General must contend
with. There's sloth in the Congress, ambition and disloy-
alty among his subordinates, a daily wasting of the
troops as the terms of enlistment run out—. To be truth-
ful, sir, we've only the ghost of an army here, and if
Howe should attack us with resolution we're done.
We've eight hundred Continentals—that's Nixon's old
brigade and what's left of the Virginia and Maryland
regiments—and some three thousand militia who are
here today and gone tomorrow. We're perishing for
want of clothing, want of shoes, stockings and blankets,
want of food even. When the men desert or go off at the
end of their terms, they take their arms away with them.
To make a show of force, we've quartered soldiers in
Whippany, Hanover and Chatham as well as here, but
the ruse fools no one. Come spring, we're promised six-
teen new regiments of foot, four of Light Horse, and
four of artillery and artificers. I'll believe in them when
I see them, for we've no money to pay the promised
bounties and the recruiting officers are at a stand. We
lack for everything but hope, Frayne—and a great man
to captain us. Though I marvel he doesn't throw in his
hand and cry quits."

"What I told him was true," replied John stubbornly.
"Will he wait for the British to march before he believes
it?"

"Sure, sure," said the aide soothingly. "But you must

remember how many accounts he hears—and how much depends on the course he elects to follow. You'll find William Burnet in the church yonder. And I hope you'll make free of my quarters 'til we find you some clothes and a billet."

The Presbyterian church, now occupied by the hospital, was a small, neat building with a high-pitched roof and a tower at one side. The church furniture had been removed from it and the sick were lying on straw, spread thinly over the bare boards of the floor. The windows were tight closed against the cold and the air within was stagnant, heavy with the odors of wood and tar smoke, unwashed bodies, and sickness. It was all too familiar.

Doctor Burnet greeted John with enthusiasm but his face clouded over when John inquired where he might find John Morgan.

"In Philadelphia, I expect," he said. "But what do you want of him? He and Stringer were both dismissed their posts not two weeks ago. William Shippen heads the department now. Aye," he went on, "you do well to look amazed but that's what the Congress has done. My father, who sits in Congress from Jersey, writ me last year that Shippen was making interest against Morgan. I like the event no better than you, and yet the Director can blame himself for his downfall. He was ever too keen on the work that lay under his nose and paid too little heed to what went on at the seat of power."

"Is Shippen here?" John asked. "Must I go before him for reinstatement?"

"Never fear for that. We've too few physicians and surgeons enrolled for Shippen to balk at a qualified man. 'Twill be only a matter of form. Besides, he's not here. According to the order book, he's at Bethlehem in Pennsylvania supervising the hospital there, but in fact he's in comfortable quarters and spending the most of his time on a grand scheme for reforming the whole medical service. Meanwhile, I'll be glad of your help. Nathaniel Bond lies sick of a fever and my mates are fit only for nursing."

He gave John a sad account of his embarrassments as they walked the rounds together. Since Congress made no regular appropriations for the hospitals, there was a constant shortage of necessaries; at the moment, sweet oil, wine, spirits, rice and molasses were all lacking. He had no cash to pay for vegetables and the sick were fed puddings of Indian meal, an occasional scrap of mutton, and grog. For want of glass bottles, the apothecary-general could not distribute the medicines he compounded, and many of the drugs themselves were unobtainable. Without hog's lard, it was impossible to make ointments.

The Morristown hospital housed only sick men, lying on the straw in their own thin, filthy clothing. The wounded at Trenton and Princeton had been carried by wagon and sledge to Bethlehem, Easton, Allentown and Philadelphia, halting on the way to spend the night in freezing barns and outbuildings whereby many of them had died. Unused to camp life, the militiamen sickened quickly, the southerners sooner than the northerners and the young sooner than the old. When soldiers fell ill in camp, they deserted rather than enter the hospital for the word had spread that a stay in hospital meant certain death. They wandered off, therefore, and if by good fortune they won their way home, they infected their neighbors with the flux or the breakbone fever. But the most of them dropped on the roads like rotten sheep.

"What can I do?" exclaimed Burnet. "A senior surgeon ranks lower, as you must know, than the youngest officer of the line. I've waited on the General with my complaints but he's as powerless as I. He refers the situation to Congress, and they to a medical committee who talk about it; and then no more is heard. Yet our trouble here is nothing to what I've been told of Bethlehem and other hospitals in Pennsylvania, where they tumble the sick and wounded together in confined places and the very air breeds disease. Do you know James Tilton who was with us lately? An excellent physician and a thoughtful man. Light, room, and clean air are the first considerations in a hospital, he says—yet how shall these be secured without help or means? I swear to you, Frayne, that the vengeance of God must surely overtake those miscreants in Philadelphia for their ignorance and their unconcern."

The sick at Morristown exhibited all manner of diseases. There was rheumatism, for which the sufferer was bled of ten ounces from the arm on the affected side and was given vinegar and water to drink; there were fevers —putrid, bilious, hectic, intermittent and breakbone; there were flux and jaundice, frostbite which often required amputation of a member, the venereal disease, and rheums of every type. A constant stir and coughing disturbed the hospital, and moans of men in pain, and crying out for drink.

"You see what we face," said Burnet when they had completed their rounds. "And I've kept the worst for the last. Two days ago, we had a death by smallpox. The

General has ordered me to inoculate all the well men but I'm fearful of the effect. We haven't enough jalap, calomel and snakeroot for the preliminary dosing. And where will we put them whilst they sicken? Not here, certainly."

"We held them under guard in private houses at Cambridge," said John. "You must do so here."

"Aye, but we've so few houses in the village—and if we shelter them through the countryside they'll give the disease to their hosts unless we inoculate them too."

"We shall do it then."

"The Quarter-master will object."

"Leave him to me," said John. "I'll undertake to persuade him—or to frighten him, which will have the same effect."

Returning to Fitzgerald's quarters in the Hoffman house, John dined off cornmeal bread, bacon, and a mug of hot rum punch. It was coarse fare but there was plenty of it, and his sense of irony was touched by the pleasure it gave him. A golden opportunity to entrap and defeat the enemy was fated to be lost; he had been suspected and rebuffed by his superior officers; he was committed to practice his profession under impossible conditions—yet he could find himself almost cheerful in the satisfaction of his hunger. A dog or a wolf was his equal in that. However, he had learned something in the stormy months since his capture—to be slow in judgment on men who erred; to understand that an error was not necessarily an effect of malice or covert treason. The gaunt, slow-spoken man in the Arnold Tavern, conning over his papers with weary diligence, might

well prove unequal in imagination to the task he had
undertaken, but he was neither a sluggard or a traitor.
Trenton and Princeton had not been accidents. With
the least of means, he had maneuvered the conquering
British into a posture of defense. Even the tragic mishap
at Fort Washington appeared in a different light to
John now, and he was no longer sure in his opinion of
it. It may have been caused, as some said, by Greene's
bad advice. But whatever the cause, the sacrifice of the
garrison had purchased time for an escape from total
ruin. Some had been lost that the most might be saved,
and Washington had withdrawn his army from commitment to an open battle which he could not win. A memory from the schoolroom returned—of Fabius Cunctator,
Fabius the delayer, whose patient strategy of retreat had
saved Rome when more brilliant captains failed. There
might even be a good reason why Congress had chosen
to supplant a wise and dedicated director of hospitals
with a clever, shallow intriguer like Shippen. The gentlemen of Congress need not be miscreants, as Burnet
had termed them; they might only be plain, dull men
who had been deceived.

Vastly weary, he pulled off his boots and was asleep
almost as his head touched the pillow.

He rose very early next morning, dressed, breakfasted,
and set off on a ramble through the village and the en-
campment. A full battalion of infantry were assembled
in marching order on the parade ground, ready to move
out. They looked spruce and well-fed by contrast with
the ragged Continental who stood beside John and

watched them too, spitting out tobacco juice at regular intervals and saying nothing. There was that about him which spoke to John of home.

"A smart looking regiment," he began. "Who are they?"

"Militia," the Continental replied and spat. "From Philadelphia. Not worth the time of day."

"Are they going on duty?"

"They're goin' home. Their enlistment's up and they're quittin'."

"They've chosen a perilous time to quit."

"They ain't alone. Mifflin's whole brigade is bent on quittin'. Day afore yesterday the Delawares went off—them as was billeted round about the Ford house."

The man looked John up and down, and shifted his quid to his other cheek.

"Seems like you're askin' a heap of questions," he said. "You a sailor?" And when John had identified himself: "From Wendham, are you? I'm a Medford man myself, and sorry I ain't there now."

"I expect you'll leave the army too, when you've served your term."

"Can't. I guv the Gin'ral my word to stay when I took the bounty last month. 'Twan't much of a bounty—only ten dollars, paper—but a bargain's a bargain. 'Most all of us in Hitchcock's agreed to it."

"Hitchcock's regiment?"

"Hitchcock's brigade, they calls it now—what's left of it. 'Twas Nixon's 'til Nixon was ordered north and Dan'l Hitchcock took the command. Dan'l is dead, though. He died soon after we set up camp here."

"Perhaps you can give me news of some of my

friends," said John. "They've served with Hitchcock's since the siege of Boston."

"Likely so," said the man and spat again. "Who?"

"Abijah Flagg?" The Continental nodded his head. "Heavy-built man in the blacksmithing trade. I recall him. But I ain't seen him since we marched south across Jersey. Dead, maybe. We lost a mort of our men on that retreat."

"Ben Ripley?"

"Him that was a friend of old Flagg's?" The soldier grinned. "A cross tyke he was, always. He quit us right after Trenton fight. He'd served his 'listment time, he said, and t'hell with the bounty and the army too. Let some Committeeman take his place, he said. As for him, he meant to go home and get him some of the hard money he'd heard was a-makin' there."

"Richard Sprague? Jesse Ware?"

The man knew nothing of them or of any other of the Wendham men who had joined the Continentals. Could it be, thought John, that only he was still in service? Sam Ellis had died at Bunker Hill, Abijah was believed dead and probably was, for he was too simple and stubborn a man to take his hand from the plough. Ben Ripley had slunk off to Wendham. Had the rest fallen on Long Island perhaps, or at the White Plains? Or had they died less nobly of cold or disease and been huddled in nameless graves? For all he knew, they too might have wearied of virtue and the cause and turned their faces homeward as many another had done. Had he not himself been tempted so? Then why not they?

Fitzgerald was waiting for him at the Hoffman house. The aide had rummaged out some clothing for him—a dress coat of bottle-green with tarnished silver lace, broadcloth small-clothes, worsted stockings, and a hat with an officer's cockade. They were all something the worse for wear but he donned them gladly.

By eight o'clock he was at the hospital. Burnet had spent the night there and John had no little trouble persuading him to go to his quarters and sleep.

"Fevers are up," said Burnet fretfully. " 'Tis because of the diet, I'm certain. I was promised milk from a farm over Whippany way but it hasn't come. The farmer's found a better market no doubt. Here are some notes I've writ down on the critical cases. None died last night, yet I shouldn't give sixpence for that lad by the wall. He has lung fever and coughs blood and hangs on to life by will alone. Keep a sharp watch on those scoundrel mates. They shirk their duty whenever they can and they're proper thieves to boot."

After Burnet had gone, John saw to it that the fires were built up in the stoves and the bathing tubs filled with hot water preparatory to a thorough cleansing of all the sick who would not be further reduced by immersion. He had just begun to read over the notes which Burnet had left him when one of the mates called out that he must come quickly—a man was dying.

It was the young rifleman of whom Burnet had spoken. By the time John reached the place by the wall where he lay, the gush of bright blood from his mouth had ceased and he was inert; his skin was hot all over to the touch and his wide-open eyes were already glazing. John knelt beside him in the straw and spoke soothingly to him, for there was little else to be done.

"Ain't Sam Williams come yet?" the soldier asked in

the soft accents of Virginia. "Sam's my cousin and he never broke a promise. He'll be here."

"So he will," said John. "He will indeed."

"He was here last night. I seen him plain as plain come through that door. 'Take cheer, Will,' he said to me. 'So soon as ye're hearty, we'll take the road again. I'll come for ye and we'll go to Kentucky to stay.' "

"Kentucky?" asked John. It was only a word to him— the name of a district, as he thought, in the wilderness west of Virginia. A strange and wonderful place it well might be, but Will would never see it.

"Aye, sir, where the Long Hunters go. Dan'l Boone is forted up there, and James Harrod is too—but the settlements ain't the place for Sam and me. We've had right enough of tidewater folks and valley folks too. We traveled our lone last year when we went through the Gap and 'long the trace through the canebrakes to the big river. We seen a new sky, and a new rich earth all covered with grass as blue as the waves of the sea. Everywhere in the woods was game—elk and deer, and so many turkeys they're like one flock. There's elm and oak and locust and pine, as tall as the trees in Eden's garden; there's dogwood and redbud too. When we got to the plains down south of the river, we hit on a lick where the critters go to lap salt. Two, three hundred bufflers was there—great cows they are, with short, curved horns—a-makin' off at a run as we come up. It's all there for a man to take—a fine, fresh land where all he does is important, where he's free, where he moves as he likes and no one'll hustle or let him but the redskins." He put out his skinny hand and tried to grasp John's wrist; his clutch was feather-light. "Ye won't forget?" he said. "Ye'll tell me when Sam comes? Right now, I'm sleepy like—"

The wild look of delirium faded from his eyes; there was a great awe and sadness in them for the moment he gazed at John before his head drooped to one side and his pulse no longer beat.

Each man that lived would be free, thought John as he closed the dead boy's eyes, but no man could define what freedom meant. To run away to the country of a dream? To stand aside from life in proud dissent? Freedom was none of these but something subtler and more austere; it was bound up inextricably with the rights and hopes of all other men. No man could ever be free as in a state of nature; the common good must be the mark of his aim, and the establishment of a wisely and fairly ordered civil community the end of his efforts. If to this end he must fight and die perhaps, so be it; such was the condition of mankind. Nor could he rest thereafter, for the worst enemies of freedom were unrelenting and were all within man himself—apathy, luxury, selfishness, and the instinct to look to others for easy solutions in time of peril and crisis. Should his countrymen win this struggle with old England—should all the vast continent of which the boy had spoken be their own at last—much, much would be required of them. The land must not be wasted, nor its wealth permitted to lull the people into corruption and ease. The fight must go on, long after the last drum-beat, and all men of conscience and reason must gird to win the peace. If they should fail, then America must fail in time as Europe had failed.

He rose to his feet and looked around him at the lines

of patient, suffering sick. If he, John Frayne, would be free, he must begin here in servitude. Let others deal with the strategies and pomps of war, they were not his work. In the Providence of God, he was skilled to save men from death and this must be his share in the grand design.